Mail Order Mistletoe

Book 17 in Brides of Beckham

Kirsten Osbourne

Visit my website at www.kirstenandmorganna.com

Chapter One

MARGARET O'REILLY TOOK a deep breath. She had the four youngest of the Miller children, not-so-fondly known as the demon horde to all of Beckham, Massachusetts, in her class, and she was ready to strangle every single one of them. Why would a seventeen-year-old boy put a snake in his teacher's desk? Why would he even think about doing something so ridiculous?

"I'm going to send a note home to your parents. I need one of them to sign it and send it back to prove that they've read it. Who wants to carry it home?" Meg asked, her voice stern and angry.

None of the four children from the family would even look at her, let alone agree to take the note. "Fine, I'll walk over there after school." She knew the children didn't want her in their home. They'd made that clear in the past.

Eventually, the youngest of the children, a ten-year-old girl named Ida raised her hand. "I'll take it home. But the others will probably throw me on the ground and take it from me before I get it there." She had her blond hair in braids, and she was the best-behaved of the four, though that wasn't saying much.

The words didn't shock Meg one little bit. She'd seen what the demon horde was capable of, and she was downright sick of them.

When the school day ended, she gave Ida the note, and made her promise to have it signed. As soon as Ida walked off, Tom, the eldest of the demon horde still in school sauntered to her desk, a newspaper in his hand.

"I'm sorry you don't like my brother and sisters and me, teacher."

Meg glared at the worst of the four. "No, you're not. You're not a bit sorry, or you wouldn't behave as you do. Please just go home and leave me alone." She was tired of looking at him.

He set the newspaper on her desk. "Since you're such a failure at teaching, I thought you might want to go see my sister. Her name is Elizabeth Tandy, and she lives in town on Rock Creek Road in the biggest nicest house you ever did see. She sends women out to be mail order brides. You know, women who aren't good at anything else, and can't find themselves husbands. She sends them."

Meg closed her eyes and counted to ten again. When she finally opened them, she was alone. In the month since she'd started teaching there, the Miller children had locked her in the outhouse and tipped it over, put three reptiles, six rodents and two amphibians in her desk, started four fist fights, done no schoolwork, and sent a letter to the school board saying she wasn't pretty enough to teach there.

Why, she didn't know. She knew for a fact she wasn't ugly. Probably just their way of trying to chase her off.

She looked down at the newspaper with the words *Grooms' Gazette* emblazoned across the top. Maybe she was stupid, but she was actually considering it. She read through a few of the ads, some were funny, but there was one that seemed downright intriguing to her.

"North Dakota farmer needs a woman for housework and companionship. Twenty-eight years old, not ugly, and has all his own teeth. See Elizabeth Tandy on Rock Creek Road in Beckham, Massachusetts, or write to Mr. Lars Borgen in SunSet, North Dakota."

"Well, if Mrs. Tandy is the older sister of the demon horde, maybe I can talk to her about her poorly behaved siblings while I chat with her about Mr. Lars Borgen," she said to the empty schoolroom. She got up and swept the floor, making sure the fire was banked before heading into town. She should have enough time to make it to town and back before it was too dark to see her hand in front of her face.

She locked the door and headed toward town, dreading meeting another member of the Miller family. Surely they weren't all as—pleasant as the ones she'd already met.

When she got to Rock Creek Road, she realized she wasn't going to be able to make it back to her house beside the school before dark. She needed to do whatever she could to get away from her terrible situation, though. The dark could be faced once. The demon horde could not be faced for a full year!

She knocked on the door of the huge house, intimidated by the sheer size of it. She'd grown up in a large house, but it hadn't belonged to her family. Papa had been the gardener and her mother the cook. They were so proud that she was teaching. Hopefully they'd understand what the demon horde was driving her to do.

The door was opened by a tall blond man. "May I help you?"

"Yes, I'm here to see Elizabeth Tandy." Meg suddenly wished she'd taken the time to wash her hands and face. She could see soot all over her hands from cleaning up the mess the children had made when they had dumped it all over the classroom to—well in an effort to cover her with soot. It had worked beautifully.

"Is she expecting you, Miss—?"

Meg shook her head. "No, she's not. It's Miss O'Reilly. I'm here about her newspaper."

The man nodded. "Right this way, Miss O'Reilly. Would you care to wash your hands and face before you see her? There's a sink right through here." He opened the door to the bathroom for her, and Meg ducked inside thankfully. She quickly washed her hands and face and stepped back out into the hallway.

"Thank you."

"It's not a problem. Mrs. Tandy is in her office." He walked to a room at the back of the hall and opened the door for her. "Elizabeth, there's a Miss O'Reilly here to see you."

Mrs. Tandy stood, and turned toward the door. Meg was immediately struck by her beauty, and her extremely pregnant state. She looked like she could have the baby she was carrying any minute.

"Please don't stand!"

Elizabeth laughed, her eyes sparkling. "I promise, the baby won't fall out on his head if I stand. Bernard? Would you please bring us some tea and cookies?"

As soon as the man had left the room, Elizabeth grinned at Meg. "I find any excuse a good one for tea and cookies at this point in my pregnancy." She patted her belly with obvious affection. "Please sit down, and we'll chat."

Meg took a seat on the couch, while Elizabeth moved to sit beside her. "It's nice to get out of that awful desk chair for a bit. You want to be a mail order bride?" she asked.

"Yes, I do. I'm the teacher at the local school, you see, and the demon horde—I mean your siblings—are amusing themselves by making my life miserable."

Elizabeth put her hand over Meg's. "I'm so sorry. My younger siblings are truly rotten to the core. I don't spend any more time with them than absolutely necessary."

"So you know?"

Elizabeth laughed. "How could I not? I lived with them. Trust me, they've done nothing to you, their teacher, that they haven't done to me. Repeatedly." She nodded at the copy of the *Grooms' Gazette* that Meg was still clutching with a death grip. "Did you choose someone?"

"Yes, him." Meg pointed at the advertisement she'd read back in the schoolhouse.

"Ah, yes. Mr. Borgen. So you want to be a farmer's wife?" Elizabeth asked with a smile.

"I want to be anywhere doing anything that doesn't involve your brothers and sisters. I would become a coal miner if I thought it would help me."

Elizabeth chuckled softly. "I don't think you'd be well-suited to that particular vocation. Let me find the letter Mr. Borgen sent me, and you can see if you still want to go to North Dakota."

She stood and walked to her desk, quickly finding the letter and bringing it back.

The door opened then, and the same man came back with cookies and tea. "Bernard, why don't you join us?" Elizabeth asked.

"Oh, I couldn't."

"Of course, you could." Elizabeth grinned at him. "I insist."

Bernard took the chair behind the desk, looking very uncomfortable. "I don't feel like it's my place to be in here when you're interviewing future brides," he said softly while Meg tried to concentrate on the letter and not on the conversation going on around her.

"It wasn't your place when you were my butler. As my husband, it's your place."

Meg blinked a couple of times. Elizabeth had married her butler? She'd assumed Elizabeth had moved there with her husband, and had married wealth. How had one of the Miller's gotten so much money?

She turned back to the letter, forcing herself to start over so she'd know what it said.

"Dear Potential Bride,

I'm a farmer in North Dakota, a beautiful state. I moved here in 1897 to be a farmer in a land that wouldn't be nearly as harsh as my homeland of Norway. Norway was a wonderful place, and I miss it a lot, but the land was not meant for farming, so it was not meant for me.

I am looking for a wife who is between the ages of nineteen and twenty-two. I would like her to be able to cook and clean well. She must not be bothered by being alone. I live a two hour drive from the nearest town, and I don't have time to run to town every few days to amuse a bride.

I need companionship and someone to cook, but I don't ever plan to fall in love with my bride. If you see yourself as a woman who will never be able to be happy without love, I'm not the right groom for you.

If you are interested in marrying me, please write me a letter. I am anxious to have a wife before winter sets in.

Sincerely,

Lars Borgen"

Meg blinked a couple of times after reading the letter. He wanted a wife but he didn't ever plan to love her? She wasn't sure she wanted that, but she could change his mind. She was sure of it! He was a better candidate for a husband than the other men she'd read about in the paper.

"I'll take him."

Elizabeth laughed, handing her a pencil and some paper. "Go ahead and write him a quick letter, telling him about yourself. It'll take about a month to get a response. No one has been interested after reading his letter, so I'm certain he'll choose you."

"A month? I have to teach the demon horde for another month?" Meg wanted to throw a fit worthy of the worst two-year-old at that news. Instead she closed her eyes. "I can do that."

Bernard coughed, obviously covering a laugh.

"Oh, don't hide the laugh. She knows they're my brothers and sisters. Rotten children that they are." Elizabeth patted her belly. "You are going to be raised with rules. I will not have a mannerless hooligan for a child. Do you understand me?"

Meg even giggled a bit at that. "Your brothers and sisters should be beaten. Often."

"I've told my mother the same thing. Often."

Meg couldn't believe she liked the older sister of the demon horde nearly as much as she did. What was wrong with her? She'd expected to hate any member of the children's family on sight.

She wrote the letter, daringly signing it, "Your future bride, Margaret." She had no idea how he'd react to that, but she had to get out. She was willing to be daring and even a bit cheeky if that's what it took.

When she finished she handed the letter to Elizabeth. "I'll send Bernard to the schoolhouse when your letter arrives. Go ahead and tell the school board you're leaving and why. I'm sure they'll have another victim all lined up before you leave."

Meg choked on her laughter. "Victim? Is that what they call teachers around here?"

"Only the ones forced to teach my younger siblings."

Bernard stood when Meg did. "I'll see you home, Miss O'Reilly. It's getting dark, and there's no need for you to walk all that way. It could be dangerous."

Meg laughed. "I just agreed to take a train more than a thousand miles to meet a stranger? What could be more dangerous than that?"

"I've investigated that stranger. I assure you, he's not dangerous as far as anyone can tell. You're in more danger teaching the demon horde. I mean, my brothers and sisters-in-law." He walked over and bent down, kissing Elizabeth on her lips. "I'll be back soon."

"Thank you," Meg said to Elizabeth on her way out.

"You're welcome. I'm happy to help anyone get away from the demon horde."

LARS STOPPED AT THE mercantile to pick up his monthly supplies and see if he'd ever gotten a response to his advertisement for a mail order bride. He'd sent his letter out more than three months before, but he hadn't had one single letter in return. Did no one want to marry a Norwegian immigrant farmer who lived in the middle of nowhere and swore he'd never love them?

He chuckled to himself as he realized just what a horrible prospect he was for a husband. Surely someone was in a bad enough situation they'd write him back eventually. He hoped. It probably wouldn't be before winter, though.

He picked out the things he needed before going to the counter to pay. "Any mail for me?" he asked, expecting the owner, George Collins, to say no as he usually did.

"Actually, yes, there is. It looks like a woman's handwriting, too!" George was the only person in town who knew Lars had sent for a mail order bride.

Lars took the letter, half expecting it to bite him. Really? Someone had responded? He opened the letter with his hand shaking a bit. He wasn't sure he could spend the winter alone again. Last year he'd almost gone insane, staring at the endless piles of snow out the window.

He read the letter slowly, and almost laughed aloud at the closure.

"Dear Mr. Borgen,

> I'm sure you were trying to scare off potential brides by saying you would never fall in love, but I assure you, after teaching school for over a month, I do not scare easily. I've had snakes in my desk and fist fights break out in my classroom. Being married to you sounds like a veritable paradise in comparison.

> I would love to be your bride. I'm nineteen years old, and my parents emigrated from Ireland before I was born. I've lived in Massachusetts my entire life, and I love it here, but I need

to be away from the evil children that I currently teach. Well, truly, only four of them are evil, but that's four too many for my taste.

I'm a good cook, and I can keep house like no one you've ever seen. I will lick the floors clean if that's what it takes to get me out of this awful school. Please say you'll take me. I'm tall and slim, and I don't make children run away screaming into the night when they see my face. What more could a man ask for at this point?

Your future bride,

Margaret"

He needed a woman who was desperate. Well, he'd definitely found one this time. "George, I need a pencil and paper to write her back. She's willing to come."

George handed him a pen and paper and watched as Lars quickly scrawled out a letter. He added some money, and then he rushed out of the store to buy a train ticket. When Lars came back minutes later, George had already boxed his supplies for him. "You need help with these, Lars?"

"No, thanks, George. I got it." He handed George his letter. "Get that out as soon as you can. I'm expecting a bride in a little over three weeks."

"Will do. And may she be as sweet and precious a woman as you've ever seen."

Lars waved on his way out, putting his supplies in the back of the wagon before climbing in to make the two hour drive home. He was thankful Margaret had answered his letter. She seemed like a woman with a sense of humor, and that was important to him. When she found out he really never planned to love her or have any tender affections for her, she wouldn't be pleased.

That was simply not to be helped, though. He'd buried his heart in his back field with his wife and stillborn son. No, there was no love left in him to give her. He'd give her children though. That's all he had left.

He thought of nothing but his sweet Olga the whole way home. They'd married in Norway before he'd found out about the railroad's offer for farmers. There weren't enough men in the West, so the Northern Pacific railroad had offered cheap package deals for farmers to buy land and get transportation all for one lump sum. He'd jumped at the chance, bringing his new bride with him.

Lars had only been nineteen when he'd crossed the ocean with Olga in tow. She'd lost the baby she was carrying while they were on the ship, and had begun to cry and beg him to return home then.

He couldn't though. How could a man pass up the opportunity to work land that was meant to be farmed? The land in all of Scandinavia had been brutal to farmers for centuries. No, he knew he was doing the right thing.

Now he wondered if he'd been closer to home when Olga had first gone into labor if she'd have lived. If their son would have lived?

No more would he worry about those things. Mail order brides were easy to come by here in the United States. If this one died, he'd just send for another. There would be no love involved. There couldn't be. Lars Borgen no longer had a heart.

He'd go visit Olga and their son later, and tell her of his plans. He knew she'd understand, though. How could she not? She knew he needed a son.

He would plead her forgiveness, even as he told her he was marrying another. He loved her too much to ever care for another. She would understand that.

Chapter Two

IT WAS MEG'S LAST DAY teaching at the school outside of Beckham. A replacement had been found, and this time they'd found a male teacher who was known for not sparing the rod, or the ruler as the case may be. He would do much better with the unruly demon horde, she was certain.

She hoped Bernard came for her soon, because she had enough money to stay at the boarding house in town for two weeks, but after that, she wasn't certain what she would do or where she would go.

Maybe she should look for a job as soon as she got off work. Surely someone in town needed a cook. She was one of the best cooks around, thanks to her mother's tutelage. She'd also make a wonderful nanny to anyone who didn't have the last name Miller. Why she'd even work for the demon horde's older sister if it came to that.

She'd spent most of her extra money for the past month working on new clothes that were more suited to a farmer's wife than the ones she wore. Her school clothes were all the latest style, and they certainly weren't right for anything but going to church for a farmer's wife in North Dakota.

North Dakota. It might as well be the North Pole. She hadn't dared tell her parents she might be leaving her post as a teacher to travel across the country and marry a stranger. No, it would be better if she wrote them after the fact. They wouldn't be pleased. Not even a little bit.

After she'd dismissed school for the day, thankful to see the backs of the demon horde for the last time, she swept the floor in the schoolroom and erased the blackboard. She meant to leave the school as neatly as she'd found it.

She was just finishing up when she heard the door open, and she turned, expecting one of the demon horde to have returned to torment her one last time.

Instead it was Bernard Tandy. "Mr. Tandy! Does this mean my letter came back?"

He smiled as he extended it to her. "It did. Elizabeth said I should wait for you to read it, in case you needed a ride into town."

"I need a ride into town, no matter what this says. Today is my last day of work, and I need to get my things out of the house provided for me, and move into town tonight. I've quit my job rather than lose my mind."

"I understand. I hope the letter holds good news for you."

Meg moved to her chair to read the letter, trying to ignore the large man prowling the room.

"Dear Margaret,

You sound like exactly the type of woman I am looking for. I've enclosed a train ticket for you, leaving Beckham, Massachusetts on Saturday, October 31st and arriving at the station in Mandan, North Dakota on November 6th. I'll be waiting for you in Mandan, and we will make the drive to SunSet to marry.

I look forward to your arrival.

Your future husband,
Lars"

Meg did her best to contain her glee. One night in a boarding house wouldn't be nearly as taxing on her finances as a week would. "I have a train ticket for eight tomorrow morning."

"Oh good! I'll give you a ride to town. Why don't you stay the night with us rather than wasting your money on the boarding house?

We have plenty of room. Of course, you'll sleep better in the boarding house, because there my son won't keep you up all night."

Meg's face lit up at the news of the baby. "Oh, congratulations! I'm so happy for you. What did you name him?"

"Benjamin. Shall I follow you to your house?"

"It's no longer mine, but yes, please. And I'd love to spend the night. I would prefer not to spend the money on the room, if that's really all right with you."

"Of course. We've had several brides stay with us, sometimes for as long as a month. It's not a problem."

"Thank you!" She finished up the last of her tasks and picked up her bag. "Let's go to the house. I am all packed and ready to go." She had only two bags, so she could have easily carried them to town, but it was already getting very cold, and she didn't want to be out past dark.

They walked next door to the teacher's house and got her two bags. She closed the door of the house sadly. It had been her first place to live alone, and she'd gotten a taste for independence. She would miss the house and the freedom it had brought.

She didn't say much on her ride to town, having little to say to the man beside her. Instead, she watched the scenery as she passed it, wondering how different North Dakota would be. She'd been raised in Boston and had never lived outside Massachusetts.

When they got into town, he drove straight to Rock Creek Road and she went in. Elizabeth wasn't in the room she'd first met her in, and instead she was in a parlor at the front of the house, holding the baby.

Meg was the youngest of the children in her family, so she had no experience with babies. She knew the basics of how to take care of one, of course, but she'd rarely had the chance to hold one. She walked into the room where Elizabeth sat on the sofa, taking a seat beside her. "Thank you for allowing me to stay here tonight. It will help me a lot."

Elizabeth frowned. "You're welcome to stay here as long as it takes for your train to leave. Bernard wasn't supposed to offer for just one night."

"My train leaves first thing in the morning," Meg said with a grin. "He's a handsome baby." She peered at the little boy on Elizabeth's lap.

Elizabeth trailed her finger along Benjamin's cheek. "I think so. I'm so happy he's finally here, and I can hold him."

"Do you want more children?"

"I want a dozen or so, but I'll be content with whatever God gives me." Elizabeth's eyes met Meg's. "I promise I will not let them act like the demon horde. I couldn't imagine."

"I was quite happy to see their backs leave my classroom for the last time today. Honestly, I've never been so happy." Meg shook her head. "I have never dreamed children that poorly behaved existed. How did you turn out all right when your siblings were so awful?"

Elizabeth shrugged. "The oldest four were raised differently. I'm the second eldest. Most of the younger ones are actually good people now that they're out from under my parents' influence. There were fourteen of us total. Mama had two more after my oldest sister was already married."

"I'm the youngest of seven, and I can't imagine acting like that."

"I know. I don't think most people can. I really am sorry. I hate it when people realize we're all related."

"Well, I promise not to think less of you for it," Meg said with a grin. "I'm actually very impressed with your business and very thankful that you found me a place to go and a man to marry. He sounds like he's a very good man."

"I'm sure he is. I have a network of matchmakers around the country and we are always checking out the men for each other, making sure they'll treat the women well." Elizabeth looked down at the baby. "Usually when I match a woman, I go to the train station with her and talk to her about marriage. I need you to know that if your husband hits you or hurts you in any way, you don't have to stay. You have the right to leave, and you would have a place back here, if only until you get back on your feet."

"Does that happen?" Meg asked, surprised.

"It could, so we tell our brides about the possibility. It hasn't so far, because we investigate each groom before sending a bride out to him."

Meg nodded. "I see. Well, thank you for the offer." She really couldn't see coming home with her tail between her legs, but she couldn't see staying in a situation where she was being abused either. She'd have to think about that when and if the time came.

"I won't be able to go with you in the morning, because I just had the baby last week."

"That's fine. I can walk. It's not far from here."

"Did you bring a lot with you?" Elizabeth asked. "Because Bernard would take you if you had a lot of things."

"Oh, no ma'am. I have two carpet bags and a small bag of teaching supplies. I don't know why I'm even holding onto them, but I guess it's so I can teach my own children some day. It sounds like the farm is way too far out for there to be a school near."

"That's probably true. If you want Bernard to walk with you anyway, he certainly will. He's done it many times when I couldn't for whatever reason."

"You must place a lot of brides."

Elizabeth laughed. "You wouldn't believe me if I told you. Why, I once placed a couple dozen women all at once, because of a factory fire. It's amazing how quickly we can find places for people when we really need to."

"I do admire the work you're doing."

"I'm pretty proud of my business. I inherited it from the last matchmaker who ran it. She herself went West and married. I'm still in touch with her quite often, but mostly I'm on my own now."

Meg stood. "I'm sure I'm keeping you from more important things. Where am I staying?"

Elizabeth gave her directions to her room. "We'll have supper in about an hour. Bernard and I would love for you to join us."

"Thank you. I will." Meg walked up the stairs and found the bedroom Elizabeth had sent her to. It was small, but very luxurious. She had never stayed anywhere so nice in her life. She wondered if she'd spend the rest of her life wanting to go back to Beckham, just because of the memory of it.

She looked through her things, wondering if she was taking too much, but really she had three dresses for working around the house, and three for Sunday. It was a lot more than she'd ever dreamed of having. She only had one apron, but she'd bought fabric for another. She could sew on the train. Why, it would help her stay busy.

There was a knock on the door, and a woman's voice called that supper was ready. Meg jumped up and hurried down the stairs, happy to be included. She'd had a lot of lonely nights in the teacher's house.

THE FOLLOWING MORNING, Meg was up well before the sun as was her habit. She dressed and made sure she had everything together for the train trip for the fourth time in the past twelve hours. It felt so unreal to her. How could she be leaving everything she'd ever known to get on a train and marry a man who was a stranger to her?

She arrived at the train station with her bags in hand at quarter before eight, praying she was ready. She'd never done anything quite so rash, so she wasn't certain how she'd handle things. She had no idea what the man looked like or who he was, but she would be his bride in just seven days. What kind of thinking human being agreed to something like that?

The woman who sat beside her waiting on her train, smiled at Meg. "You seem nervous. Have you never been on a train before?"

"I have been on a train, but only once. I'm nervous because I'm going to be on a train for seven days, and then I'm going to marry a stranger. I don't know what I was thinking to agree to do this!" Meg stood up, looking around for an escape. She sat back down a moment later. She couldn't go back to her position as a teacher, because it had already been filled. She wouldn't anyway. The demon horde was not made up of children. They were beasts.

The older woman laughed. "You never really know a man until you've been married to him anyway. You'll be fine." She patted Meg's hand. "I was a mail order bride back in 1867, right after the War Between the States. My father died in the war, and my brother couldn't support all of us, so I went out West as a bride. I settled in Minnesota, and married a kind, loving man. We've been married for almost thirty years."

"Oh, that's wonderful! Is he with you?"

The woman's eyes grew sad. "No, I was here because my mother grew ill. She died two weeks ago. It's not good news that she died by any means, but it does mean that I can now return home to John. I've been here for three months taking care of her."

"I'm so sorry about your mother."

"Thank you, dear." The woman forced a smile. "I'm Gertrude, by the way. My friends call me Gertie."

"And are we friends?"

"We're about to have a long train ride together, so I certainly hope we are going to be!"

Meg laughed. "I'm Margaret, but my friends all call me Meg."

"Meg. I like that. It suits you well."

Their train was called then, and they both stood. "I'm not sure I'm ready to be on a train for this long." Meg was almost as nervous about the long train ride as she was about the marriage.

Gertie smiled. "Trust me, it's better than being on a wagon for that long. You have to get out and walk beside the wagon, and when it's your turn to drive, your bottom gets so sore. No, this is a much better way of traveling. It's so much faster!"

Meg nodded. "I shouldn't complain about riding on a train. I know it's so much better than what people did even sixty years ago. This new age we live in is simply amazing."

"It is. I'm glad you can recognize that."

They found seats beside each other, and Meg settled into the trip. She pulled out the pieces of the apron she'd cut out and a needle and thread, determined to keep busy for at least a portion of the trip.

"While you work, tell me what made you decide to be a mail order bride. That's not something every pretty young lady just gets up and does."

Once Meg started talking, she couldn't seem to stop. She told about working hard to get her teacher's certificate, and how proud she was. Then she talked about her first school, there outside Beckham. "The children were mostly well-behaved, but there were these four children from one family..." Meg realized she had a captive audience, and she detailed every prank the children had played and every fight they'd fought. When she got to the part where the oldest of the demon horde had laid the *Grooms' Gazette* on her desk, Gertie gasped.

"I've never heard of such horribly behaved children. I hope you got your ruler out and took that boy to task!" Gertie said, fire in her eyes.

"I considered it, but he was seventeen. He was at least six inches taller than me, and he was used to farm chores. He would have hurt me!"

Gertie shook her head. "It's not right that you were expected to deal with children like that on your own. What did the parents say?"

"I never could get them to come in and talk to me. I considered going to their house after school, but quite frankly, I was afraid to." Meg shook her head. "I never thought I'd admit that I was afraid of my students, but I was. And I could only imagine the parents being much worse. I mean, they were the ones allowing them to run wild that way."

"I don't know what you'd have run into there. So you went to their older sister?"

Meg finished up her story and sighed. "I haven't even had the courage to tell my parents that I'm off to North Dakota to marry a complete stranger. I know they wouldn't be pleased with me."

"No, they probably wouldn't. Why I'd be furious with my daughter for doing the same thing, even though I was a mail order bride myself. It just doesn't seem like something my daughter should do. Back then it seemed the ultimate adventure. I don't know how safe it would be in today's world." Gertie frowned. "When you get to North Dakota, and you meet your Lars, you send me a letter straight away so I know you're there and you've arrived safely, and he hasn't hurt you or anything. I don't want to get home and worry about you nonstop."

"I promise!"

Gertie immediately wrote her address on a piece of paper, giving it to Meg. "May I help you make something?" she asked, eyeing Meg's project.

Meg shook her head. "I only brought enough fabric for one apron to work on. I should have gotten more."

"That's all right. We can chat while you work."

By the time Gertie got off the train six days later, Meg had not only finished the apron, she had written long newsy letters to her parents about what she'd done and she had written each of her siblings. She had read two books and spent many hours staring out the window.

As Gertie's stop was called, Meg got to her feet, hugging the older woman tightly. "I'm so glad I got to know you. I will write as soon as I know he's not planning on murdering me in my sleep. I hope you don't mind having a pen friendship with me."

"Mind? I insist! You're a special young lady, Meg. Don't let anyone ever tell you differently."

Both women had tears in their eyes as they parted ways. A woman who had watched the two of them for a couple of days from the vantage point of the seat across from Meg, asked, "Was that your grandmother?"

Meg laughed. "She's my new friend I met just before we got on the train in Massachusetts."

"I could have sworn you were related by how close you were."

"We were strangers a few days ago." Meg frowned. "I feel like she's always been a part of my life now, though."

Chapter Three

LARS SAT IN HIS WAGON, waiting for the train to arrive. He was nervous, and he didn't want to be. There was no reason at all for him to be nervous when he didn't plan to have feelings for the woman. She would be a partner of sorts, a woman to keep his house, cook, and warm his bed. Emotions were unnecessary between them.

She'd said her name was Margaret, but he had no idea what she was like other than that. He hoped she was pleasing to the eye as well as a good cook. A good cook was more important at that point. He'd lost a great deal of weight since his wife had died.

He frowned as he thought of Olga, thrusting her from his mind. He couldn't think of her when he was about to meet his new wife. It wasn't right, no matter what the relationship he would have with his new bride.

The train pulled up and he strained, trying to see his new wife. Only three people got off the train, two women and a man. The man took the older woman by her elbow and led her off, leaving a young slender woman with long dark hair and dark eyes standing alone on the platform.

Lars jumped down from the wagon and approached her, watching her closely to see if she seemed to be looking for someone else. He stopped in front of her, his heart in his throat. "Margaret?" he asked.

Meg looked up at the man in front of her, liking what she saw. His hair was a darker blond than she'd expected from a Norwegian man, and his eyes were a slate gray. "Yes. You must be Lars."

"Ja. I'm Lars." His voice was heavily accented with Norwegian.

"It's nice to meet you, Lars. My friends call me Meg."

"Meg," he said, trying her name out for himself. He'd gotten used to thinking of her as Margaret, so Meg seemed awkward. "Well, Meg, let's drive to SunSet and we'll meet the preacher there."

"How far are we from SunSet?" Meg asked as he took her two carpet bags and carried them toward a wagon.

"It's about an hour drive, and then we'll drive another two hours to get to my house."

"I see." She really would be stuck in the middle of nowhere with no one but him for companionship. She wondered idly if he had a pet she could talk to during the day. All the way there, she'd been worried about the kind of man Lars was. She got there, and she worried about loneliness. Would she be able to stand being alone so much?

He put her carpet bags in the back of the old farm wagon, before helping her up onto the seat. He ran around the wagon and took his spot beside her. "After I sent the letter, I worried that you would get it too late to be on that train," he said, looking for something to talk with her about.

"I had less than twenty-four hours to get ready, but the timing was really good. My last day of my job was the day before I left."

He looked at her from the corner of his eyes, sitting so primly with her hands folded in her lap. She'd been on a train for seven days, and she still looked fresh. How on earth had she managed that?

"Was your journey pleasant?"

"It was good, and I was dreading it. I met a woman old enough to be my grandmother at the train station in Beckham before I left, and we sat together. She told me stories, and I told her about my students and about coming out here to marry you. We're going to be pen friends."

"Do you like writing letters?"

She shrugged. "I do. I have several people I'll be corresponding with regularly. It brings my friends to me from far away."

He considered that for a moment. "I should probably spend more time writing to my family back in Norway. They would enjoy hearing from me, but I work long hard hours. It's hard to have energy at the end of the day."

"Well, some of the things you've been doing for yourself, I'll be able to do instead. It will be a bit easier, I think."

"Maybe." He drove on in silence, not really knowing what to say. He didn't really want to get to know her well. She was going to be a very small part of his life.

Meg tried to come up with something to say, but nothing came to her mind. Lars seemed to be a man of few words. She didn't know if she liked that or not. Instead of talking, she stared out at the endless prairie. There were few houses, and none together. There weren't really very many trees. It was beautiful, but very different than Massachusetts. She missed the ocean already.

Finally, after a long period of silence, she saw a few houses clumped together. "That's SunSet," he said. Nothing else, just the name of the town as he drove toward it.

Meg wondered if she was crazy to go through with this wedding. Maybe she should run once they reached town, but he'd spent a lot of money to get her there. And really? He was a good looking man with impeccable manners. They didn't have much to say to each other, but they were strangers. Why would they?

Lars stopped the wagon in front of the small church where he'd attended services a few times with his wife, Olga. He shook his head, banning her from his mind again. The preacher, Pastor Green, was expecting them, and they needed to get a move on.

He walked around the wagon and helped her down, feeling how tiny her hand was in his. She was a tall woman, but he was a very large man. Taller and broader than most, and even though he'd lost weight, he still weighed at least half again what she did.

"Pastor Green is expecting us."

Meg took a deep breath, trying to still her nerves. What was she thinking marrying this stranger? "All right." She forced a smile, wishing he were at least a bit more personable. The few words they'd exchanged told her nothing about him.

He led her into the church, and she saw the preacher standing at the front talking to an empty room. Practicing his sermon, most likely.

"Pastor Green, this is my bride, Margaret. I told you to expect us this afternoon?"

Pastor Green, an older man who had more hair on the sides of his head than on top of it, smiled at Meg. "Are you ready to be married to this crazy Norwegian?"

Meg smiled. "I think so."

Pastor Green laughed. "I wouldn't be sure either if someone wanted me to marry Lars." He picked up his Bible and faced the two of them. "Let's get started."

The wedding vows were kept short and sweet, and Meg heard herself answering when she was supposed to, but she had no idea how she managed. When it was over, the pastor said Lars should kiss his bride.

Lars looked at her skeptically, wondering if she'd run if he brushed his lips across hers. He leaned down and very gently touched her lips with his, and she stared at him afterward, as if she had no idea what she'd just done.

He ignored her skittish look for a moment and turned back to the pastor. "Thank you, Pastor Green. We appreciate your time."

Taking Meg's hand, he led her across the street. "I've requested enough supplies for a month be waiting for us at the mercantile but there's a diner here. It's not much, just three tables, but they serve good food. If you're hungry, we'll grab some food before we get our supplies and get on our way."

Meg nodded, following him into the building. They took a table to one side and someone came out to them. "You want beef stew or fried chicken?" the woman asked.

Meg was surprised by only two choices. "Beef stew please." She was hungry and a good stew sounded so much nicer to her than something greasy. Normally she didn't mind, but after so long on trains when all she had were the sandwiches sold there, she was hungry for some real food.

Lars nodded. "Make that two please." After he'd ordered, he looked down at the table where Meg's hands rested. He should probably hold her hand while they ate, but it would seem forced. "I'm glad you went through with it."

Meg's gaze met his, hers full of surprise. "You didn't think I would?"

"I wasn't worried about it until you arrived, but you seemed so nervous."

"I just traveled halfway across the country to marry a stranger. I'm entitled to be nervous." Why couldn't he see it was a normal reaction?

"I understand that. I meant what I said in my letter." He knew his wedding day wasn't the time for this discussion, but he needed her to understand. "I'm never going to love you."

Meg took a deep breath. She hadn't expected him to be so blunt. "I hope you know I'll do everything I can to change your mind about that. I don't like the idea of a loveless marriage."

"Why did you marry me then?" he asked, confused.

"There was no one else in the paper who appealed to me. You did. I figured if I couldn't change your mind, then I deserved a loveless marriage for thinking I should."

"Well, I want to be clear about what I'm looking for from you." He didn't know how to respond to what she'd said, so he'd just go on with the discussion. "I want someone who will keep my home clean, cook meals, and keep me warm at night."

Meg nodded, having expected that last part. "You'll give me some time to get to know you first?" She knew she was asking a lot, but she needed it. When she'd answered his advertisement, she hadn't realized she would, but he intimidated her a great deal.

He frowned. "I wasn't planning on that. We're married. I have rights." He didn't need just a cook and housekeeper. He had physical needs, and as his wife, it was her duty to take care of them.

"One week is all I ask. I want to know you a bit better. I want to feel comfortable with you before I—let you do that to me." She fumbled over her words, very embarrassed to be having this conversation with him.

"Let me? You're my wife. It's your duty."

She took a deep breath. "I realize that, and I plan to fulfill that duty. But I'd like a little more time to get used to you before we do that."

"I suppose a week won't hurt me," he said grudgingly. "But no longer than a week. And during that week, I plan to kiss you whenever I feel like it."

"I—whenever you feel like it? What if I'm busy?"

"What could you be doing that was more important than kissing your husband?"

She envisioned removing a roast from the oven and burning them both. "You won't do it when I'm holding something hot?"

He laughed. "I won't endanger either of us to kiss you. I'm not a stupid man."

Their food arrived and was slid in front of them.

"I don't think you're stupid. I think you were very smart to warn whoever came here to marry you that you had no intention of ever loving her. Most women would have been scared away." All *intelligent* women would have.

"Well, you weren't, and I'm glad. I need a wife. I can't spend another winter alone."

"Is that the main reason you wanted a wife?" she asked. "Companionship?"

He shook his head, not willing to lie to her. "I want a son. I want sex. I want decent meals. In that order." He knew his words were blunt, and he watched her to see if she'd run off. They were married, but an annulment would be easy at that point.

She sighed. "I see." Getting this man to fall in love with her would really be a challenge. It was a good thing she adored challenges. She took a bite of her stew with a grin. He wasn't going to know what hit him.

AFTER LEAVING THE DINER, they stopped at the mercantile where the owner had a small tower of supplies stacked. "I didn't get just your usual this month, Lars. I went with everything a newlywed couple usually needs."

Lars nodded. "Thanks, George. I appreciate it." He looked over at Meg. "This is my new wife, Margaret. Meg, this is George."

Meg smiled and nodded. "It's nice to meet you."

"I look forward to seeing you for the monthly supply orders."

Meg frowned looking out on the prairie. "What if the snow is too deep to come out?"

"We'll bring the sleigh," Lars said. "You can stay home if it's too cold for you, but I can't miss my supply runs. I have George put in extra in case I'm a week late due to weather, but we can't go much longer than that."

Meg wondered what would happen if they were trapped out on the prairie with no food, but she didn't ask.

Lars seemed to read her mind. "If we were stuck out there, I would hunt for food. There's always something to shoot, or I would kill one of our milk cows if it got terribly bad, though I'd prefer not to."

"I see. So there's always a plan if something goes wrong."

"Of course. I've lived here for eight years now. I know what I'm doing. Mostly."

George laughed at that. "He knows pretty well how to keep alive."

When the wagon was loaded, Lars and Meg left town and headed toward the farm. "It's about two hours from here. You can sleep if you need to."

She shook her head. "That's all I did for the last twenty-four hours on the train after my new friend left."

"What was your friend's name?" he asked. He wouldn't get to know her any better by asking her about the stranger she'd made friends with on the train. That would give them something to talk about without bringing them closer together.

Meg told him everything she knew about her new friend, Gertie, as they drove. "I wish she didn't live so far from here. She is a kind woman, and I'd love to learn more from her."

"You'll find we live far from everyone. The closest farm is a twenty minute drive."

"Oh." Somehow she'd imagined there would be someone close enough that she could walk to their home and talk to them. Apparently not.

"Are you disappointed?" he asked. "I said in the letter that I was isolated."

"I guess I didn't realize just how isolated you were. It's going to feel like we're the only two people on earth. Do you go into town on Sundays for church?" she asked.

He shook his head. "I can't drive four hours just to sit in a church building for two hours. It doesn't make sense."

"No, I guess it doesn't. I will miss church, though."

He frowned. "I wish it were some other way. Maybe more people will settle, and we can start a church out here."

"Maybe." She looked at him, considering. "I have never eaten Norwegian food, so if you are wanting me to cook that way, I'll need a cookbook or something. Otherwise I will cook what I know."

"Anything you cook will be better than anything I've tried to cook over the years. I'll be very happy with anything you make for me."

He glanced at her with a slight smile. "Thank you for thinking of my heritage. I do appreciate it."

"I thought about buying a Norwegian cookbook and learning some dishes before I came, but I didn't know how to do that." She shrugged. "How did you come to be in North Dakota?"

He briefly told her of how he'd been a farmer in Norway, and how hard it was. He'd been trying to farm wheat, just as his father had tried to farm wheat. There just wasn't enough farmland in all of Norway. "So when I saw an advertisement offering land and an inexpensive trip to North Dakota, I jumped at it. It was a wise decision." And he still felt it was wise, even after what had happened to Olga and their son. He knew someday he would need to tell her about Olga, but he didn't feel like their wedding day was the right time.

"It's already getting very cold here," she said, snuggling into her coat. She was glad she'd worn it. "I was hoping it would be a bit warmer than Massachusetts, but I didn't expect it to be."

He laughed. "Any land with the word north as part of the name cannot be expected to be warm."

She shook her head. "North Carolina is quite warm! I had a student from there, and she talked often about how cold Massachusetts was in comparison."

"Tell me about your time teaching," he said, looking for a way to keep her talking. He found he enjoyed listening to her, but he had no desire to tell her about his own life. She might be able to stay distracted that way.

She told him a series of stories that had him laughing harder than he remembered laughing for a long time. Maybe since he left Norway. "And people really call these children the demon horde?"

"Yes! There's no other way to describe them! And for me the funniest part is their older sister, Elizabeth, is the one who sent me here to marry you! She is a lovely woman and a matchmaker. She's truly made something of herself. She told me that the oldest four children in the family were actually well behaved, and it was the youngest ten who made up the demon horde. All of the ones who are grown have become good people. They're married and work hard. I cannot imagine any of those children I taught doing anything but causing problems. They were bad. I was almost afraid to walk into my classroom, because I never knew what was going to happen when I did."

"I have a hard time believing that children who behaved so badly could grow up to be anything but disrespectful, rude adults. It seems odd to me. And yes, it's strange that Elizabeth is their older sister. Who would have thought? Does she have children?"

Meg smiled. "She had a son a couple of weeks ago. It's their first."

"Oh, that's nice." He didn't look at her, afraid she'd see the intense longing for a son to take over his land in his eyes. He'd already told her he'd married her primarily to get a son, so she shouldn't have a problem with it.

Chapter Four

WHEN HE WAS CLOSE ENOUGH for her to see the house, he stopped the wagon, and took her arm, pointing into the distance. "Do you see a small house over there? The chimney is visible. The house is made of wood, and it is painted white." He never would have painted the house white, but he knew it's what Olga wanted, and he did everything he could to keep her happy. He wouldn't pander to the whims of his new wife the way he had his first.

"Oh, I see it!" It was little more than a speck off to the distance, but she could see it. Her new home. She couldn't remember the last house she'd seen, so they would truly be as isolated as he'd said. She'd hoped he was exaggerating a bit, but apparently not.

"How much longer before we get there?" she asked.

"About fifteen minutes. You can see far on the prairie without trees to block the way."

"I'm going to miss having trees all around me. Massachusetts has trees everywhere."

"You'll get used to it. It's a nice place to live." He shrugged. "The farmland is so much better here than it ever was back home in Norway. I'm glad I made the long journey."

She sighed, wondering how long it would take her to be able to say she was glad she'd moved west, if ever. He seemed like a kind enough man, but there didn't seem to be any warmth or emotion about him. It made her sad to know he was the only person she'd see every single day for years to come. Yes, they'd occasionally go into town, but that was a long journey. She wanted to have a friend close by.

She kept her eyes peeled on the house, looking at it carefully, wanting to know everything about it. It was beautiful from here, and it was bigger than she'd imagined it would be. Was it two stories? She couldn't tell from there.

When he finally stopped in front of it, she wanted to jump down on her own, but she sensed he wouldn't like that. She was used to getting in and out of wagons on her own, but she wasn't used to being married as she did it. "Your house is lovely."

He smiled, thankful for the comment. When she got inside, she wouldn't feel the same, he was sure. He wasn't good at keeping the house tidy like Olga had, and he hadn't done dishes in a very long time. He hoped she didn't get as angry as she probably should.

"You go in. I'll follow with your bags," he told her. He didn't want to see the disappointment on her face when she saw how filthy the house was.

Meg hurried ahead, throwing the door open, and taking a deep breath. There were dishes piled all over the kitchen, and there was dirt all over the floors. It had obviously once been loved by someone, because there were curtains at the windows. They were dirty curtains, but they were curtains.

She wandered through the house, seeing that there was not only an upstairs, but there was a proper staircase. It wasn't a ladder leading up there. She told herself to be thankful for the good things, and not fuss over the mess.

There was one bedroom at the foot of the stairs and she looked into it. It was obviously his. The sheets were quite dirty and there were clothes all over the floor. The first things she would need to do were laundry and dishes. Before those two tasks were handled, she wouldn't even be able to really get started on anything else.

There was another room there on the bottom floor, and she looked into it. It was relatively clean, except for the dust on everything. It was a parlor, and she could imagine spending happy evenings there, crocheting or sewing while he did whatever men like to do in the evenings.

Her days would be full for a while at least. That was good. It had to be.

She climbed the stairs to find two bedrooms at the top. One looked like it was meant to be a spare bedroom, complete with an unmade bed and a dresser. The other room was a nursery. She frowned. That nursery had a great deal of dust on it. Why would a single man build a nursery as soon as he built the house? Surely he'd wait until he had a wife.

And then it all clicked in Meg's mind. He'd been married before. That's why the house had once been loved by someone. That's why there was a nursery. And more importantly, that's why he said he would never love again. It all made sense to her now, even though she didn't want it to.

She climbed back down the stairs slowly, not sure how to broach the subject with him, so she didn't. He'd gone into his bedroom and closed the door, so she removed her coat, pulled her apron over her dress, and rolled up her sleeves. If she could do even a portion of the dishes tonight, she would be able to get more done tomorrow.

Lars came out of his room wearing work clothes. "I'm going to go out and milk the cow and gather the eggs. I will be back."

She was pleased to hear she'd have fresh eggs and milk every day for her cooking and baking. She watched him go, a sad look on her face. How long would he wait before he told her about his lost wife?

She stood at the sink, thankful for the water pump. She wouldn't have to make trips out to the well to do dishes and laundry, and that would make her life much easier than it would have been.

By the time he was back from milking the cows and gathering eggs, she'd made serious strides in the work at hand. She had many of the dishes washed, and all the pots that had food caked on them, which was all the pots in the house, were soaking. She wiped off the table and scrubbed out a skillet. They'd had a late lunch, so he didn't know if he'd want to eat again that night. If he did she could make some bacon and eggs or some pancakes.

"Are you hungry?" she asked as he set the milk on the table and put a basket of eggs beside the pail. "I could make something simple tonight like bacon and eggs or pancakes."

His eyes lit up. "Pancakes? It's been a really long time since I had pancakes." He went to the boxes he'd carried in from the mercantile and found some flour and some maple syrup. "George knows I love maple syrup." He had gotten a new bottle every month when he picked up supplies while Olga was still alive.

She smiled and nodded. "Pancakes it is." Looking around she found the other ingredients she'd need. She took a mixing bowl she had just put away and quickly mixed the batter, spooning four circles onto the large skillet.

He looked around the room. It was already looking much better than it had in two years. She'd done a good portion of the dishes and cleaned off the table. He'd gotten into the habit of moving the dishes around on the table and eating in smaller and smaller spaces until he was forced to do dishes or eat from pots.

When she set the first plate of pancakes in front of him, he wished she'd had time to make butter in the churn, but because she hadn't, he picked up the syrup and covered them. Then he leaned in and just smelled them. It was going to be a treat not to eat his own cooking. Apparently she knew how to cook some of his favorites as well.

She made pancakes until the batter was gone, refilling his plate twice. Finally she sat down with the last two pancakes and a glass of milk for herself. "Do you like French toast as well?" she asked.

"What's that?"

She shrugged. "It's just a way of using up older bread. You dip the bread in a mixture of milk and eggs and then you fry it like you would a pancake. You serve it with butter and syrup."

"If it has syrup, I will eat it." He didn't know why he had such a love for all sweet foods, but he did.

"Then I'll make those when I need to use up bread."

"That won't happen."

She frowned at him. "Why not?"

"Because I haven't had fresh baked bread in so long, I don't think I'll be able to stop eating it once I start. It sounds delicious, though."

She laughed. "I'll make a bit of extra and hide it, just so I can make you some French toast. How would that be?"

"It sounds lovely. I should have married a long time ago, just so I could eat good food again."

"I'll do my best to keep you happy." She hadn't taken the time to dig through all the supplies from the store yet, because she didn't want to put them into a dirty kitchen. She'd clean out the pantry and make sure everything was spotless before she started to put the food in there.

When he'd finished eating, he leaned back and patted his belly. "That was delicious. Thank you."

She smiled, getting up and taking both of their plates to the sink, and immediately started another round of dishwashing.

He watched her, wondering when she'd start berating him for the mess he'd left, but she never did. She did every dirty dish he had left out, drying them and putting them away. Then she took all the pots she had soaking and she washed the ones she could easily wash. She set the others onto the stove. "I'll have to boil those to get the food off, and that can wait until tomorrow. For now, I'm tired."

He got to his feet. "If you still want to sleep alone, there's a bedroom upstairs you can use. You're welcome to share my bed, of course, but I can't promise I won't touch you."

"I'll use the bed upstairs for tonight, thank you." She smiled at him, wondering how she was supposed to say goodnight to the husband she'd met only a few hours earlier. Really, it was out of her realm of experience.

Lars caught her hand, pulling her toward him. At her wary look, he shook his head. "I just want to kiss you goodnight. You did say I could kiss you whenever the mood struck me."

She nodded, raising her face to his, expecting the same slight brush of the lips he'd given her in church.

He cupped her face in his hands, leaning down and touching his lips to hers. When he'd kissed her in the church, there'd been no real spark between them, and as much as he didn't want to love the woman, he did want the passion she could show him.

He lifted his head after a very brief kiss, rubbing his thumb over her lower lip as he looked into her eyes. "Have you ever been kissed before?"

She nodded. "You kissed me at the church, remember?"

He chuckled softly. "That wasn't a real kiss. That was just a touch of my lips on yours. Have you ever had a real kiss?"

"I'm not sure what you mean." Why wasn't that a real kiss?

"Let me show you." His head lowered again, and this time his lips played with hers. His tongue stroked her bottom lip, seeking entrance into her mouth.

Meg was unsure what he wanted, but when she parted her lips to ask, his tongue swooped in, showing her in a way that was much more effective than any explanation ever could be.

Lars let out a groan, his hands moving from where they still cupped her cheeks to her tiny waist as he pulled her flush against him. There was the spark he needed. He wanted her badly. He wanted to drag her into his bedroom and demand his rights as a husband, but that was no way to get her to acquiesce.

No, he'd take things slowly, and when he did make it into bed with her, she would want it as much as he did.

Finally he lifted his head, his forehead resting against hers. "Now do you understand the difference?"

Meg nodded, slightly out of breath. "I—had no idea people kissed that way." She was embarrassed to admit it, but at least he would understand how inexperienced she was. "Goodnight, Lars."

"Goodnight, Meg." He touched his lips to hers briefly. "I will see you in the morning."

He walked off toward his room, wondering how he was going to keep his heart from being taken by her. He'd thought he had buried it with Olga, but his lust and his love were too closely knit. He shut the door softly behind him, trying to force his heart to stop its erratic beating.

He would have to quit thinking of her as anything more than a housekeeper and cook, a vessel for his seed. She would bear his son, but she would get no affection.

Outside his room, Meg stood frozen. She had felt more from that kiss than she'd ever imagined was possible. He'd touched her lips, her heart, and her soul. How on earth could a man make her feel so much in such a short time?

She slowly climbed the stairs to her empty room. She couldn't find any clean sheets, so she put a quilt over the mattress, and folded it in half, lying on half and covering with the other half. She didn't bother changing into her nightgown, knowing she wouldn't be warm enough. It was warmer downstairs near the fire.

She lay for a while with her eyes wide open staring at the wall. What would life be like when she allowed him more than a kiss? He was hiding so much from her, denying his first wife and a child, she was certain. She understood why his heart was off-limits to her, but she wanted him to voice the words to her. Telling her would be the right thing to do, and he seemed like such a good, honest man who always did the right thing.

When she closed her eyes, she saw nothing but his face. His eyes as they looked down into hers. Her lips still tingled from his touch. She could feel on her sides where he'd gripped her waist. Never had she thought she would be attracted to a man like him. A good little Irish girl was never interested in a man who wasn't from the Emerald Isle.

While her family may be disappointed in her for marrying, and especially for marrying a Norwegian man she'd never met, she didn't care. Something about the sad, lonely man touched her heart. Sure, she had a lot to do to take care of him, and to get his house in order, and he was so brooding he could easily make her crazy, but one touch and she melted like sugar in his arms.

She only hoped she would be able to hold out for a full week, and take the opportunity to get to know him as she wished. Maybe it was folly on her part, but she felt that once that part of their marriage started, the courtship would end, and she desperately wanted the courtship.

Meg had always dreamed of a man who would sing her love songs, who would bring her flowers. She had never met a man willing to do either, but now she'd married, she had a chance for it to happen. At least, she hoped she did. He seemed to be so distant from her, except when they touched.

He was willing to share his body with her, but she could tell he would need persuasion to share his heart. She was an Irishwoman at heart, and she firmly believed that a man's heart should be held firmly by a woman before she agreed to spend a night in his bed. There was no hope of getting him to agree to such a thing. No, he wanted to hold himself away.

She could only do what was within her abilities. She'd clean and cook for him. She would make his home a place where he could be proud to bring people. Anything beyond that was impossible. Perhaps she could find a tender spot by making special meals for him, or cleaning up the things his first wife had put out everywhere. Maybe that was what it would take.

Maybe making sure he knew she respected his feelings for the woman who'd come before her would be all it would take. It was hard to know, because she barely knew him, but that wouldn't continue. She would not spend her life married to a stranger. Meg Borgen was going to have the love of her man. She didn't care what it took.

Once she'd decided on a course of action, she finally closed her eyes. Tomorrow she would make him love her.

Chapter Five

MEG WOKE EVEN EARLIER than usual the following morning, convinced that if she showed him how hard she would work, he would realize he could love her. She tiptoed down the stairs and quickly made bacon, eggs, and pancakes for breakfast. She wouldn't always go overboard on everything, but she would until he started to love her. She knew she could make it happen.

She put a pot of coffee on, assuming he drank it because it was in the supplies, and set the table. She looked around the kitchen at all that was left to do in just that room. She needed to scrub the floor, several pots, and the walls. The stove needed to be blacked badly. She was certain it hadn't been done in at least two years.

She yawned, wishing she could go back to bed just thinking about it all. Today would be a day for cleaning the kitchen, baking bread, and doing laundry. She wanted every piece of laundry in the house clean and on the line before noon. It may not be possible, but she was certainly going to try.

She had breakfast on the table, just as the front door opened. She jumped, startled.

"Got fresh milk and eggs," Lars said, setting them on the work table. He walked to her and kissed her softly. He didn't sink into the kiss as he wanted to. He needed to keep his distance, and kissing, for whatever reason, made him feel more for her. How he'd talk her into his bed early without kissing her a lot, he didn't know, but he'd figure that out. Soon.

"Breakfast is ready," she said with a smile. "How do you take your coffee?"

"Black," he replied, watching as she poured his coffee into a cup and set it beside his plate. She'd gone all out for breakfast. He couldn't remember a time someone had fixed both eggs and pancakes for the same meal, but he certainly wouldn't complain about it. It all looked delicious.

"I'll try to find time to make butter today, but I think there are other things that are a little more important.

He sighed but nodded. "I do have some food in the cellar. There are some canned goods I purchased a while back, and some potatoes and some carrots. Maybe even a pumpkin or two if you like pumpkin pie."

She took her seat across from him, grinning. "So you want me to make pumpkin pie? Is that what you're saying?"

He shrugged. "Only if you like it, of course." He wouldn't ask her to go out of her way to make something special for him, because he wouldn't ever return the favor. He couldn't.

"Of course. Any apples down there?"

He shook his head. "Apples are hard to come by around here. I've planted some of the seeds I've gotten when I bought them from George in town, but they haven't grown much yet."

"You'll need to show me where they are, so I can do my best to fertilize them and keep them going." She took a bite of her eggs, watching him as she ate. "What kind of farmer are you?"

Lars frowned. "A good one, I hope."

She shook her head. "No, I mean what do you grow?"

"Oh, I'm a wheat farmer. This is good land for wheat."

"I see." She didn't know much about wheat except that it was ground to make flour. "Is there anything in particular you're hungry for? Anything you want special for supper tonight?"

He shook his head. "We'll worry about special meals after you've had some time to get the house where it needs to be. I've been seeing a lot of deer, so I might bring you one so you can make some stews. Do you know how to dry meat?"

"No, I don't. If you show me once, I can learn though."

"I have a spring house I use for keeping meat fresh. I'll show you before I go out today. Then you can choose what you want to fix." He finished the last of his breakfast, wiping his mouth on the back of his sleeve. "Are you finished?"

Meg looked at her plate. No, she wasn't nearly finished, but she'd go with him. "I'm ready."

She followed him outside, and he explained the buildings to her. "That's the chicken coop," he said of a small sod building. "The chickens wander in and out, but I've used some of the new barbed wire to keep predators out as best I can."

He showed her a small barn, this building made of wood. "I keep two cows in here, and my four horses. I have two teams. One is mostly for driving and the other is for farm work."

"I see. Will I need to feed the animals?"

He shook his head. "The only outside work I'll ask of you is to keep a kitchen garden come spring and summer. You'll grow most of the food we eat. It'll save us a lot of money at the mercantile in the fall and winter."

She nodded. "I expected that."

He took her to the well. "We have the pump in the kitchen, but if it acts up, just come out here and bring water up from the well."

"I can do that," Meg told him. She hoped she'd have time to churn butter that day, and she'd work quickly to make it happen if at all possible. She could make a simple stew for supper to take less time so she could manage it.

He took her to the other building that was again made of mud. It was barely tall enough for him to fit into. "This is the spring house. I rerouted a bit of the stream through here to keep meat cold enough. I got fresh meat in town yesterday. George got it from the butcher and added it to our order. I brought it in here before going into the house last night."

She looked around the building, noting the meat in the water. She rubbed her hands over her arms to warm them. "Is there anything in particular you want me to get started on today?"

He shook his head. "There's a lot to do, and I appreciate you being so willing to get started. Do what you can and leave the rest."

Meg nodded, watching as he walked away at those words. He was off to work, and she was expected to do her share now. It was a good thing she'd bought a pioneer handbook back in Massachusetts before she left. It wouldn't tell her everything of course, but it would get her started. "Wait! Will you be home for lunch?"

Lars turned around. He didn't want to come home for lunch. He didn't want to see her that often, but he would be hungry. "Yes, I'll be home for lunch today. After today, I'd appreciate if you could pack a lunch pail for me."

"Of course!"

Meg hurried into the house to get the dishes done. She'd start the stew right away and make it big enough they could eat it for both meals that day. She'd make him sandwiches for lunch tomorrow. She could be a wife. She just needed to learn what he expected of her.

She hurried into the house and finished her breakfast, before doing all the dishes that were left. She was able to scrub out the rest of the pots after they'd soaked overnight, and she put a large one on the stove, before hurrying out to the springhouse to find some meat. When she stepped into the small building, she shivered again. It was just as cold in there as it was outside and it was almost freezing outside.

She found what looked like beef to her, and she carried a two pound portion into the house, and chopped it into pieces. She put it into a large pot, and added enough water to cover it, wanting the meat cooked before she added the vegetable for the stew.

She then put a pot of water onto boil for the laundry. She was not looking forward to dealing with all of the dirty clothes and bedding, but it had to be done first. She stripped the curtains off the windows, and even found a tablecloth wadded up in one of the kitchen cabinets. She spent over an hour with a scrub board, thankful she didn't have to beat her laundry against a rock. She hadn't been sure he would have a scrub board, but after a bit of searching she found it. Apparently his wife had everything she'd needed to do her job well.

Once everything was hanging on the line, she hurried back into the house and down to the cellar, carrying up potatoes and carrots for the stew. She peeled and cut up the potatoes and carrots and seasoned the water, mixing a little flour with water and adding that in to the pot to thicken it. She smiled, looking down at it. It would be perfect, and ready by the time he came in for lunch. She glanced at the clock and saw it was already ten-thirty, and she felt like she'd accomplished so little.

She took everything out of the pantry and scrubbed it, carefully deciding where she would put each of the things they'd purchased at the mercantile. When she had it just like she wanted it, she scrubbed the fronts of the cabinets and the table again. She'd put the table cloth she'd found on the table before supper, and it would start to feel like home.

Glancing at the clock she saw she still had thirty minutes before he should be there for lunch, assuming he'd eat at noon. "I wish he'd told me what time he'd come back, but at least lunch will be ready whenever he makes it." She talked to herself as she mixed up bread dough, kneading it on the work table. She made enough bread for three loaves, draping a towel over the mixing bowl so the dough could rise.

She cleaned up the small mess she'd made mixing the dough, and washed her hands. She hated how much bread dough clung to her hands when she was baking.

By keeping busy, she'd been able to keep her loneliness at bay. She really hoped she could get some kind of pet, so she wouldn't be alone all the time, but that was something they could discuss at a later time.

For now, she had enough work to do that she shouldn't even notice the loneliness.

Lars came into the house at half past twelve, sniffing deeply. Something smelled wonderful. When Olga was alive, he'd have rushed to her and hugged her, telling her how good it smelled. "Something smells nice," he said, knowing he needed to compliment her work, even if she wasn't his first wife.

Meg turned from her spot at the stove. "I'm glad you think so, because this is lunch and supper today."

Lars walked to the sink and washed his hands, using the cake of soap on the edge of the work counter. He was happy to see she was a woman who kept her surroundings clean. He'd had no idea what he was getting when he asked for a mail order bride. "I could eat that for lunch and supper every day for a week and not tire of it."

She grinned. "Maybe you should try a bite before you say that."

He shrugged. "It smells good, and I'm not a picky eater. I wouldn't have survived eating my own cooking if I was." Sitting at the table, he waited for her to bring him a bowl of the stew.

"What would you like to drink with lunch? I can make more coffee or milk? Water?"

"Water is fine for lunch. I prefer milk with supper and coffee with breakfast." He waited as she put the water in front of him, and took a big swallow. "When you make my lunch tomorrow, send me out with a couple of jars of water as well. I'll need them."

Meg nodded, serving herself some stew and a glass of milk. She sat opposite him and took a bite of her stew, smiling with pride. It tasted as good as her mother's. That's all she cared about with a stew. "What did you do this morning?" she asked.

He frowned at her. He shouldn't have to talk about his work. "I plowed the fields, so they would be ready to plant in the spring. I try to get everything done before the first snow flies."

"Has there been snow here yet?" she asked curiously. They'd had one snowfall in Massachusetts before she left, but it hadn't been a big one.

"Not yet. Soon." He ate quickly, ready to get back to his plowing. "I'll finish work by about six-thirty." He told her, standing and putting his hat back on. "I'll see you then."

He walked out of the house without even thanking her for making his lunch. She made a face. If he couldn't be even a little bit thankful for her hard work, she might have to get angry with him. Of course, she hadn't thanked him for plowing the fields to earn a living for them, so maybe he needed to be shown what she expected. She'd do that later.

Meg did the lunch dishes, punched down the dough, and put it into bread pans to rise again, carefully covering the pans with a towel. Then she got back to work on the house.

After scrubbing the kitchen floor, she turned to the walls, washing them briskly. She'd wait to blacken the stove. It needed it, but she had too many other things that were more important.

Walking outside, she checked the clothes on the line, realized they weren't dry enough to take down yet, and then she went back inside. She found the butter churn in the corner of the kitchen and frowned at it. It was much too dirty for her to be able to use. She cleaned it out, and then got the cream from the last couple of days that was saved in the basement. Thankful they even had a basement to keep things cool, she poured the cream into the churn and began the long process of churning the butter. She'd helped her mother do it more than once, but she'd forgotten that her arms would begin to ache well before the butter was ready.

When she was finished, she put the butter into two bowls and poured the buttermilk into a pitcher. She wasn't fond of butter milk, but if Lars was, she wanted him to be able to have it. If he wasn't, they could pour it over the chicken feed.

She put the bread into the oven, and went down into the basement, getting a pumpkin. She knew he wanted pumpkin pie, and though she wasn't a pumpkin pie lover, she would make sure he had some. She'd even take the cream from the cows that evening to make whipped cream to top it with.

She sang to herself as she got the meat of the pumpkin out, cutting it into chunks. She'd never actually made a pumpkin pie, but she had it in her recipe book. Before she moved out of her mother's house, she'd been presented with all of her mother's recipes written down for her in a notebook. She was thankful for that now, though she'd thought her mother was being silly at the time.

She removed the bread from the oven, smiling at the perfect loaves. It was her first time to bake bread without her mother standing over her, so she was happy it had turned out so well. Back in Beckham, it had been easier to buy her bread from the baker in town than make her own. She'd had the extra money to do what she wanted, because her house had been provided. The small school had paid more than most, but she understood as soon as she started why it had. They knew the kind of children they were asking her to deal with.

Meg sighed and pushed her failure as a teacher from her mind. She'd never realized just how badly she would feel leaving the job half done.

She finished up the pie and slipped it into the oven, smiling to herself. Already having accomplished more than she'd intended to do all day, she went back out to get the clothes in off the line. They were finally dry, thanks to the strong wind blowing across the prairie.

While she was removing a sheet, she heard a soft animal cry from the direction of the house. She walked over and found a tiny kitten, barely old enough to be weaned hiding under a bush. She picked it up, holding it close. "I bet you'll be a good mouser in a few months, but more importantly, you'll be a good companion now. Why don't you live with me?" She snuggled the kitten under her chin, giggling when its fur tickled her. "What should we name you?" She thought for a moment. "That's it! I'll call you Beth. Beth was everyone's favorite in Little Women, and she was Meg's little sister. I was named after Meg, so you can be named after Beth."

She slid the kitten into the pocket of her skirt and went back to the clothesline, removing the rest of the laundry. "You can help me with my chores and keep me company all day while Lars is out working."

She made up both beds with fresh sheets and blankets, thankful to have something clean for her bed. The quilts were clean too, and she wouldn't feel dirty as she slept under them. There was no better feeling in the world than sliding between fresh clean sheets.

The kitten followed her as she made up the beds, and Meg giggled as she learned to climb the stairs. Beth was afraid to follow her when she went back down, so she scooped her up and carried her.

She spread the table cloth over the table and hung the curtains back on the windows. The house looked a great deal better already, and she hadn't had any time to start on the small parlor at the back of the house or the bedrooms yet. She wasn't sure how he'd feel about her cleaning the little nursery, but she was going to do it. There was no way she'd let another inch of dust accumulate on it. Her own child would sleep in that room someday.

Chapter Six

WHEN LARS CAME INTO the house at the end of the day, he stopped short, not believing everything his new wife had accomplished. Why, she had worked as hard as he had that day, and he hadn't thought that was possible. The table was set, and the pretty tablecloth Olga had made was gracing the table. It even smelled clean.

"You've worked hard today."

Meg turned to him with a smile. "I did. All of your clothes are clean. You won't have a hard time finding anything to wear." She planned to do just a bit more laundry the following day, because of the clothes they were both wearing. She wanted everything clean. She knew it was silly, but she didn't want to have to deal with the filth she'd dealt with that day ever again.

"I'm impressed. I know women's work isn't easy, but you've done so much you make it look simple." He sighed. "I'll be ready for dinner as soon as I've milked the cow." Just as he turned to leave, he heard a soft meow. Turning back, he frowned. "Was that a cat?"

She nodded. "I found a kitten in the bushes. She seemed hungry so I brought her inside."

"I'm not really fond of cats." He didn't hate them, but found them relatively useless.

"You live on a farm. I've seen a mouse here, and the cat will take care of mice, and she'll keep me company. I don't think I can get by well without some kind of pet. At least until children come."

He frowned. "I suppose you can keep her."

"Thank you!" she said, a huge smile on her face. "Do you like buttermilk?"

He blinked a few times, trying to understand her question. "Not particularly."

"I'll let Beth have it then."

"Beth?"

"The kitten. I was named after Meg in Little Women, so I named her after Beth. You know, the sister who died."

"I have no idea what you're talking about, nor am I sure I want to. I'll be back with the milk." He walked outside, closing the door behind him.

"Well, he's a grump this evening," she told Beth. Pouring some of the buttermilk into a saucer, she giggled as the kitten put a paw in the middle of the milk as she lapped it up. "You're just going to make a mess and have to wash your foot."

The kitten ignored her in favor of her treat, and Meg hurried as she finished the meal preparations. She had the bread and butter on the table when he came back in, and she served them each a large bowl of stew.

Lars set the milk on the counter and washed his hands, eyeing the tabby cat. "She's not a very delicate eater." He grinned as she splashed milk onto the floor.

Meg grinned. "She's still a baby. I'm surprised she's old enough to be weaned. She's drinking milk just fine, though."

"You mentioned buttermilk. Does that mean you made—." He trailed off as she pointed to the butter on a plate in the center of the table beside a loaf of fresh bread. Without thinking about what he was doing, he grabbed her and kissed her with a loud smacking sound. "I have missed fresh bread more than anything!"

Meg laughed. "I'll make sure you always have fresh bread if it makes you happy."

He sat down and immediately cut himself a piece, slathering butter on it. "Delicious," he said, his mouth full of the bread. He took a swig of his milk and sighed. "I needed this."

"Well, enjoy it then." She ladled stew into two bowls and put one on the table beside his arm. "I'd like you to eat some stew as well."

"I won't forget the stew. You're a good cook," he said, cutting off another piece of the bread.

"My mother was a cook for a wealthy family back East. I grew up helping her in the kitchen, and when I left home to teach, she gave me a book with all of her recipes written in it."

"No wonder you cook so well. Do you know how to make cakes and pies?"

"I can make anything. My mother filled the book with many different desserts. And I'm what she called a 'natural cook.' I just seem to know which spices go together to make things taste good."

Lars smiled. "I'm happy to hear that. I will not complain if you want to make something new every night, or if you make this stew every day for a year. Thank you."

The words made Meg's stomach flutter. "Thank you for working all day. You're going to be an easy man to please where food is concerned, and I'm grateful for that."

When he'd finished his first bowl of stew and fourth slice of bread, she asked, "Do you want more stew, or do you want a piece of the pumpkin pie I made?"

He seemed torn. "How about another bowl of stew, and then three pieces of pumpkin pie?"

She laughed softly. "I can make that happen." She got to her feet and filled his bowl, bringing it back to him. "How did the plowing go this afternoon?"

"Very well. I'm just about finished. I should be able to do the rest tomorrow, and then I can start working on building more fences."

"Why do you build fences?" she asked.

"To keep predators away. I don't want animals in my fields."

"That makes sense." She looked over at the kitten who had curled up in front of the stove for a nap.

"Are you planning on keeping her inside?" he asked.

"I don't know. What do you think? I definitely want her to be inside some, because I want her for companionship, but I don't mind if she goes outside to hunt at night."

"That little ball of fluff is not ready to hunt." He frowned. "Keep her inside. We can let her out when she wants to go, but there's no use worrying about her getting carried off by a wolf or something."

Meg hadn't thought of the danger the kitten could be in if she was outside. "That's a good idea. She can sleep with me."

He sighed. "You're going to treat her like a baby, aren't you?"

"For as long as she is a baby, she'll be treated as one." Meg didn't care what he thought. Beth was her baby for the time being. She got up and went to the counter, carefully skimming the cream from the top of the milk so she could make whipped cream. A few minutes later, she turned back to Lars, a generous piece of pie with a large helping of whipped cream on a plate for him, along with a fork. She placed it on the table, and watched as he pushed his empty bowl away and picked up the fork, pulling the pie closer.

Taking one bite, Lars let the flavors explode in his mouth. The woman could cook and bake like nothing he'd ever seen. Why, she was a better cook than his own mama back in Norway.

He noticed that she didn't bother with a piece of pie, but instead started right on the dishes. "You don't like pumpkin pie?" he asked.

She shrugged. "I don't like it much. I'd rather save it for you, since you like it. I'll bake a cake in a day or two, and I'll certainly eat my share of that."

Lars sighed. "Thank you for making me something that you wouldn't have made for yourself. That means a lot." He didn't want to feel like she was doing special things for him, but he couldn't deny it. "You should make things that you like as well."

"Oh, I will. I could just tell you were really hungry for a pumpkin pie, so I wanted you to have some."

She put a plate over the top of the pie plate to keep the pie fresh for the next day. "I'll put a piece in your lunch tomorrow as well."

"I'd like that." He thought about his decision to eat while he was out, started to tell her he'd changed his mind, but thought better of it. He needed to keep her off his mind while he worked. Love was not in his plans. It couldn't be.

"Do you want another slice of pie? Or can I wash your plate?"

He looked down at his plate, considering. "I would like another slice if you don't mind."

She grinned, happy that he enjoyed it so much. "Happy to do it." She put another slice on his plate, and again added a generous spoonful of the whipped cream. "What's your favorite dessert?"

"Pumpkin pie. Cake. Anything sweet really. I would eat sugar by the spoonful if I thought I could get away with it."

She laughed. "Any sweets you don't like?"

He thought about that for a minute and finally shook his head. "Not that I know of. I'm willing to sample a wide variety to try to find one I don't like, though."

She grinned at that. "I'll see if I can help you do just that."

After she'd finished the last of the dishes, and he'd finished his last slice of pie, she sat down at the table with a book, wondering what they would do in the evenings. There were only a couple of hours before they needed to go to bed, but would he want to talk?

He pulled out a knife and a block of wood, and started to carve huge chunks out of it, not speaking.

She sighed, and read her book, wondering if they would always have so much silence between them. "I'm going to take the kitten outside for a minute or two."

He nodded, not glancing up. As soon as she'd shut the door behind her, he let out a sigh of relief. Too much time in her presence was not good for him, not when he didn't have the right to carry her off to his bed yet. She was too pretty for his own peace of mind.

When she came back, the kitten cradled in her arms, she said, "I think I'm going to go upstairs for the night. I'll read in bed."

He stood, walking to her. "I haven't kissed you goodnight yet."

She gave a low laugh. "I wasn't sure you even remembered I was here."

He frowned. "I know where you are every second. I don't want to, but I do." He pulled her to him, ignoring the kitten's angry cry and kissed her hard on the lips. "You're welcome to share my bed if you don't want to go upstairs."

She shook her head. "Thank you, but no. It doesn't feel right."

"Is it going to feel any righter in six days when your time is up?"

"I hope so. I really do." Meg turned and climbed the stairs. She'd done what she could that day. If a man would really fall in love with a woman because of her cooking, then she would have him eating out of her hand in a matter of days. He seemed to be a great deal too stubborn to love her for anything, though. How was she going to live in a loveless marriage for the rest of her life?

THE NEXT MORNING STARTED the same. She made pancakes and bacon for breakfast, happy that she could offer him butter for his pancakes. She knew he preferred them that way. The kitten happily drank more of the buttermilk while she worked on the pancakes.

She wasn't surprised when Lars came in from outside with the milk and eggs this time, because she had expected it. She knew he was one to rise even earlier than she did. She placed his pancakes on the table, along with a cup of coffee, while she continued to make her own. She had already put his lunch into a lunch pail and covered it with a napkin to keep it from getting bugs or dust in it.

"Will you be home around the same time tonight?" she asked when she sat down to eat her own breakfast.

He looked at her over his coffee cup. "Yes, same time. Breakfast was good." He pushed away from the table, walked around the table to kiss her softly, and took his lunch pail with him.

When she heard the door close behind him, a tear escaped her eye. He really wasn't ever going to love her. At least, that's the way it seemed at that very moment. As much as she wanted his love, maybe she should just resign herself to the fact it could never happen.

She shook her head, doing her best to get rid of the negative thinking. She didn't know where that had come from. She'd only known him two days. Of course, he didn't love her yet. How could he? He hadn't heard her sing. And more importantly? He hadn't eaten her muffins. She'd bake him some muffins that very afternoon, and then he'd come to her, begging her to love him. She knew he would. No one could resist her muffins.

She spent the day cleaning the bedrooms. Her heart was heavy as she dusted the nursery, setting it to rights. When it was clean enough for her future baby to sleep in the cradle, she knew she was done. She looked at the tiny little clothes stored in the chest there, and she knew that his first wife, whoever she was, had spent many hours preparing for a baby who hadn't lived. Her heart broke for her husband, and she promised herself she'd be patient. She had to be. She'd lose him otherwise.

She carried the kitten up and down the stairs, but she let her follow her around the rest of the time. She went to the spring house for more food and found a ham, carrying that into the house. She could make ham and some scalloped potatoes, something her mother had called one of her own special dishes.

She carried her ham into the house, the kitten trailing behind her. While the ham was baking, she peeled potatoes, and got them ready. They could go into the oven much later, but she liked for the cream to be soaked into the potatoes before she put them into the oven.

She had tucked the clothes that needed to be mended into a basket and carried them into the parlor. Taking out her needle and thread she went to work on them. If she could make the clothes he had now stretch for a bit longer, she would get the fabric she needed to make him new clothes when they were in town next. She didn't know what his financial situation was, but she had some money of her own saved from her time teaching.

She patched a few pairs of his britches before it was time to put the potatoes in the oven. She hoped he didn't mind eating day old bread with his supper, because she'd had so many other things to do that day, she hadn't gotten around to baking any.

She would use whatever was left to make him some French toast in the morning, hoping he liked it as much as she did.

When Lars came into the house that night, he sniffed the air and sighed. "Are you going to spoil me like this every day?" he asked.

She smiled. "I'm certainly going to try. You work very hard, and you deserve to come home to a meal you can enjoy." She was just sorry she hadn't made him muffins yet. The next day she would, she promised herself.

"Soon I'll be too fat to work with the way you feed me."

She laughed, eyeing his lean frame. "You'd have to gain weight to be considered thin."

He made a face at that. He'd always been lean, but he didn't like to have it thrown in his face. "I will do my best to get fat to please you."

"You already please me. You don't have to change a thing. I just don't want you to worry about getting fat, because I don't see how you could."

He grabbed the milk pail and stomped out of the house, not certain why he was angry with her. Was she trying to fatten him up? Or was she really happy with how he looked? And did it matter that much?

As he milked the cow, he wondered why he cared about her opinion. Certainly she didn't care if he was thin or fat. She'd agreed to marry him sight unseen. He was being overly sensitive. He wanted to be angry with her, and not care for her. He needed to quit looking for reasons to get angry. She was a good woman who was doing everything she could to please him, even though he'd told her that he had no intention of ever falling in love with her.

He shook his head, suddenly annoyed with himself. Meg was a good woman, and she deserved his respect, not his animosity. He needed to go back into the house and apologize immediately.

He didn't want to, but he knew it was the right thing. She was working so hard to please him, and all he did was get angry and push her away. It wasn't her fault his wife had died. No, he needed to quit treating her as if she was the enemy.

Chapter Seven

LARS WALKED BACK INTO the house with the milk and set it on the counter before turning to his new bride. "I owe you an apology."

Meg blinked at him a couple of times, unsure what he thought he'd done wrong. "For what?"

He sighed. "I've been doing everything I can to...well to not like you. I know that sounds ridiculous, and it *is* ridiculous."

"But—why do you want to dislike me? That doesn't make any sense to me at all. I'd think you'd want us to get along well." They would be each other's only companions for years to come, not counting any children who happened to come along. What good would it do either of them to not like the other?

"I do! I want you to like me, and put up with my bad behavior, while I dislike you. Ridiculous isn't it?"

She nodded as she served their meal, unsure what he was trying to say to her. "Yes, it is."

He washed his hands and took his place at the table, looking at her. "I don't want to like you, because I'm afraid if I like you, it'll be easier to love you. And I feel like I'd be betraying someone to love you."

"Your first wife?" she asked, knowing the woman needed to be acknowledged. "Why didn't you ever mention her?" Her voice was soft as she asked, but her hurt came through.

"How did you know?" he asked, surprised.

"Bachelors don't care about tablecloths. They don't care about curtains. More importantly, they don't have fully made up nurseries in their homes. What was her name?"

He frowned. Of course she'd known as soon as she went to the second floor of his house. She wasn't stupid. "Olga. We married right before we left Norway, and she had a miscarriage on the ship on the way over. We were sad, but we knew God would bless us with another baby. And He did. And that baby died too. Olga lost five babies, and then she had a pregnancy that lasted. She went into labor, and I rushed her to the mid-wife who lives about thirty minutes from here. I didn't want to risk her losing one more baby. The mid-wife did everything she could, but she lost them both."

"I'm so sorry, Lars. I know that must have hurt you."

"More than I could ever say. So I promised myself, and Olga, that I'd never love again." He frowned staring down at his food. "I don't ever want to love again. I thought I'd send for a woman, and she wouldn't want love either, because why else would she answer my letter, when I said I didn't want it? I was sure she would come here, and nothing would matter to me, but having a son. I could be happy that way."

"And I came along demanding that you will love me whether you like it or not," Meg said with a self-deprecating grin.

"It's more than that. I didn't expect to be able to like the girl who stepped off the train and into my life. I thought she would be hideously ugly and not able to find a man to marry. Instead, I find a pretty young woman who simply couldn't handle teaching a schoolroom full of hellions any longer." Lars shook his head. "It would have been so much easier for me if you were the hideous woman I expected. I could have easily forgotten about you when I went to work for the day."

"And you can't forget me?" Meg found she really liked that idea. She wanted him to think about her while he was away from her. What woman wouldn't want that?

"Of course, I can't. You've single-handedly made my home livable again in a fraction of the time I thought it would take. You've adopted a stray kitten with more warmth than I've shown anyone in two years."

"When did she die?"

"February of 1895. Just under two years ago."

"Why did you decide to marry if you wanted nothing to do with a wife?" she asked. That was the one part she couldn't understand.

He frowned, taking a sip of his milk. "I want a son. I came here from Norway imagining building a grand empire that I could leave to my sons. I have no one. It's hard being out on this lonely prairie day after day and night after night. Imagine how much harder it would be if you were totally alone."

She shuddered. She needed a kitten just to get through the hours he was gone. Imagining what it had been like for him after Olga's death made her want to cry. "I don't want to," Meg told him simply.

"So you do understand how it was. I would get up early and go to work, so I wouldn't have a chance to be lonely. I even went to church a couple of times, hoping there would be news of someone moving near, but there never was. If I had neighbors down the road, it would be different, but this prairie sucks your life away. After spending two years alone on the prairie, it started to feel like a jail. I couldn't take another winter alone. I needed to have someone to face it with me."

Meg reached out and took his hand in hers, trying to give him comfort. "Then let me face it with you. We may not be in love. We may never love one another. But we can face it as friends and companions, and maybe love will grow from that."

Lars nodded, feeling like he'd just run the gauntlet. Never in his life had he bared his soul the way he'd just done with Meg, and she'd been wonderful. He brought her fingers to his lips. "Yes, let's face it together."

She felt like they'd made a sort of peace, and she was happy with that. "I've gotten most of the house cleaned," she said, changing the subject to one that would be easier for him. "I want to clean the basement tomorrow if you don't mind. I'll probably rearrange some things, so they'll make more sense to me."

He shrugged. "I don't mind that at all. Do what needs to be done." Why would he care if she rearranged the basement?

After finishing the supper dishes, she started to go up to her room with a book, but he stopped her. "Come sit in the parlor with me," he said. "We'll talk and get to know each other better."

Meg blinked in surprise, but she nodded. "I'd like that a lot." She was very surprised at his attitude reversal, but she had no complaints about it at all. It was nice to have a husband who actually wanted to spend some time with her.

They went into the parlor, and he sat on the sofa, patting the spot next to him. "I won't bite," he said with a grin.

She laughed and took the spot right beside him on the couch. She wasn't worried that he'd bite, but she wasn't certain just how much touching she was willing to do. "I'm not afraid of you."

He chuckled, his arm going around her shoulders. "Tell me where you grew up."

She was surprised at the question. He was acting like he was courting her all of a sudden, and she wasn't quite certain how to react. With him it was either treat her like the enemy or like he was courting her. How was she supposed to know which one it would be?

"I'm the daughter of Irish immigrants. My mother was the cook for a wealthy Boston family, and my father was the gardener and handyman. We lived in a small house behind the mansion of the family they worked for. There were seven of us, and Mama often took us girls to help her work after school or on school holidays. The boys worked with Papa. I'm the youngest, so I was last at home. I think Mama was happy when I finally moved out."

"You do? They didn't like having children at home?" Norwegian families were large and usually very close knit, and he'd thought it was the same way with the Irish.

"Oh, they loved me. Don't get me wrong. My eldest brother was already married when I was born. I was a bit of an afterthought and a big surprise to my parents. They thought they were almost done raising children when I came along."

He grinned. "A good surprise, I'm sure."

"Oh, sure I was. But they were tired after all those years of child rearing, and then they got me." She smiled. "They were very good to me, and I was a happy child. I loved to go with mother to work and help her cook. She always told me I'd make some man a wonderful wife someday, because cooking came so naturally to me."

"But you were a schoolteacher?"

She shrugged. "I wanted to be independent for a while before I married. I was certain I would be a stronger woman because of it. So I moved to Beckham and taught there. I thought I'd teach for a year or two, and then I'd be willing to marry. It never occurred to me that my first school term would be so awful." She shuddered. "The demon horde was something else. I didn't mind the frogs in my desk. The lizards were bad, but I could deal with those as well. The snakes got me. And the mice! Oh, the day they put four mice in my desk, I was ready to climb atop my desk to get away from them. When I shrieked all of the children laughed. It was hard to keep their respect, when they'd heard me scream like a little girl."

Lars did his best not to laugh aloud at the picture she painted. "And so you answered my advertisement."

"Oh, it was so much worse than that! The oldest boy from the family who was still in school came to me after class one day to tell me what a horrible teacher I was. And he put a copy of the Grooms' Gazette, the newspaper his sister, Elizabeth Tandy publishes, right there on my desk. He told me since I was so useless as a teacher, I should become a mail order bride. There was nothing left for me in Beckham."

"He didn't! The boy should have been beaten!"

"Yes, he should have. Instead, I read through the newspaper as soon as he left. And I saw you asking for a bride, and there was something about your words that made me want to marry you and no one else."

"So you answered my letter, even though you knew you'd never settle for a man who didn't love you?" Lars was still baffled about that.

"I was convinced I could change your mind, you see. I'm not sure how was I was going to change your mind. That part was always very fuzzy in my head, but I knew I could."

He shook his head at her, turning her to face him more fully. "With kisses maybe?"

She blushed. "I'd never been kissed. How could I think I was so good at kisses that I could make a man fall in love with me?"

"Practice makes better."

She giggled. "Practice makes perfect."

"Oh, there's no perfect way to kiss or do anything else. Practice will make you better though." He used his index finger beneath her chin to turn her face up to his. "Want to practice?"

Meg swallowed hard. Looking up into his eyes, all she could think about was letting him kiss her. She wanted that kiss so badly. Her tongue snaked out to wet her lips, and when he still didn't kiss her, she frowned at him. "Are you ever going to kiss me?"

He laughed. "I was waiting to find out if you wanted me to."

Instead of waiting any longer, she caught the front of his shirt in her hand and pulled him down to kiss her. She opened her mouth for a deeper kiss just as he'd taught her, her hands moving over his broad shoulders. She was surprised at how much she'd grown to look forward to each kiss from him.

Lars pulled her tightly against him, half onto his lap. He splayed his hands over her back, touching as much of her as he could. He felt her corset through her blouse, and immediately wanted her to take it off. He hated corsets. They kept a man from being able to feel the woman in his arms.

He drifted one hand around to the front of her, cupping her breast in his hand and squeezing it gently.

She stiffened in his arms. No one had ever touched her there. She wanted to protest that it was something he shouldn't be doing, but she didn't know. It felt wrong, but he was her husband.

Finally, she gave herself over to the sensations. His fingers weren't hurting her. They felt good against her breast. She moved her hands over his hard back, surprised at how strong he felt. The man was so lean, probably from living off of his own cooking, but he was strong. She could feel his muscles rippling beneath her fingers.

She wanted to see him with no shirt on, but she knew it was wrong to ask. Did what was right or wrong matter just then, though? She pulled back from his kisses, looking up into his face. His lips were moist, and half open, and his eyes looked—sleepy wasn't the right word, but she wasn't certain what was. His eyes looked heavy-lidded and sexy.

"Lars?" Meg asked softly.

He opened his eyes and looked down at her. "Yes?"

"Would it be wrong of me to take your shirt off? I want to touch you."

He shook his head. "We're married. Nothing we do, as long as we both want to do it, is wrong."

"Oh." She thought about that for a moment. "Well, I want to take your shirt off and touch you. Do you mind if I do it?"

He chuckled. "I don't mind one bit. In fact, I'm sure I'll like it."

She carefully unbuttoned each of the buttons at the front of his shirt. "Do you think I'm too forward?" she asked as she applied herself to the task.

He shrugged. "Maybe, but I like it." He liked watching her face as she slowly exposed more and more skin. "Do you want to touch me?"

She nodded, pushing the shirt off his shoulders.

He stood up, pulling the shirt out of the waistband of his pants and dropping it to the floor. He sat back down on the couch, and she smiled, her hands going to the muscles she'd just uncovered. "You're so strong. I can feel it even through your clothes."

He smiled. "I thought you were calling me weak earlier when you mentioned how thin I am."

She laughed. "Weak? You?" She shook her head, touching him reverently. "I could never call you weak. I'm amazed at how strong you are." As she ran her hands over him, she wondered how her bare skin would feel against his. She'd liked his hand on her breast, so would she enjoy his skin against her breasts?

She decided not to be shy. She could find out very easily if she liked him to touch her. She knew he wouldn't complain.

Lars was startled when she jumped to her feet, but he watched as she swiftly unbuttoned her blouse, pushing it off her shoulders and onto the floor. She reached behind her to untie her corset laces, and then she dropped the garment he'd been so annoyed with just moments before onto the floor as well. She removed the only thing remaining, a thin petticoat that covered her top half, and set it on the sofa.

His eyes grew wide. His little bride was much bolder than he'd expected her to be. His gaze was immediately drawn to her breasts. They were perfect. Small, but her nipples were a pretty pink that made him want to taste them. He reached out, and his thumb flicked one of her nipples, and she blushed.

"I thought it would feel better with no clothes between us, and I was right."

He grinned. "You like it when I touch you?"

She nodded, her eyes serious. "Very much. I feel all tingly when you kiss me, and I was sure the tingling would get even worse if you touched my bare skin." She sat down facing him on the sofa, just like she'd been. "I was right."

"I like it better with no clothes between us as well."

"I want—" She broke off, certain that she was being much too forward, and he was going to get angry with her any moment.

"What do you want?" He was fascinated by her excitement over touching him.

"I want to feel your chest against mine." She felt her face flaming, and she was sure she was blushing profusely, but she kept her eyes on his.

He smiled. "I want that too." Catching her waist in his hands, he sat back against the sofa, and pulled her astride him, so they were facing one another. Her breasts were flattened against his chest as he caught her lower lip between his teeth, nipping at it gently.

She sank into his kiss, her lips parting. Her hands stroked his bare shoulders, and she wiggled a little against him, liking the feel of his hair-covered chest against her nipples. She knew she was doing things her mother would never approve of, and she had to keep reminding herself she was married to this man.

His hands moved to her hair, and he began to quickly remove pins from it. Her long hair fell out of the bun she'd contained it with, and he combed his fingers through it. "I love your hair," he whispered against her lips.

She sighed, her fingers going to his hair as well. "I like yours, but you need a haircut. We'll do that soon."

He grinned. "You're going to cut my hair?"

"If you'd like me to." Her mother had always cut her father's hair, so she was pretty certain that was common practice.

He nodded. "I'd like that. I like to feel your hands on me." Taking a deep breath, he said exactly what was on his mind. "We have two choices right now. You can either go upstairs right now and go to bed, or you can go to bed with me. If you sit on me like that for even another minute, I'm going to drag you off to my bed, whether that's what you want or not."

Meg bit her lip in indecision. "I think I should go upstairs. I—I need another day or two."

He sighed, catching her waist and putting her on her feet in front of him, silently cursing himself. He could have made love to her if he hadn't asked, and he knew it. He stood up, kissing her one last time, and feeling her press against him. "Goodnight, Meg."

She sighed as he hurried from the room. "Goodnight, Lars," she said to the empty room.

Chapter Eight

WHEN LARS CAME INTO the house with the milk and eggs the next morning, he put his arms around Meg from behind, kissing the side of her neck. "Hey no kissing when I'm messing with hot things! Remember?"

"I remember no kissing if I was going to put either one of us in danger. No?"

Meg felt hot enough she wouldn't be surprised if she'd been burned, especially where his lips were against her neck. She didn't think that would be an appropriate thing to tell him though. "Don't make me spill!"

He wrinkled his nose when he looked at what she was making for breakfast. "Oatmeal?"

She grinned. "Trust me. It's not your mother's oatmeal. It'll keep you warm while you work in the cold wind today."

"I'm going to come home for lunch," he told her.

"You are?" She turned in his arms and her gaze met his. "You don't have to."

"I remember how lonely Olga used to get while I was out working. She'd beg me to come home for lunch, and I did every day, even when it was inconvenient." He took a deep breath. "It's convenient for me to come home, and I crave the company. I'll be here for lunch." The truth was, he enjoyed spending time with her, and he realized there was nothing wrong with that.

She smiled, resting her hand on his shoulder. "I'd like that."

He leaned down and kissed her, his lips telling her how he'd missed her when she'd gone up to her room the night before. "I finished all my plowing yesterday, so I could always spend the day in bed. Of course, I'd need company for that."

She thought about it. She wanted to make him happy, but she really did want to get to know him better first. "We'll do that soon."

"How did I know you'd say that?" He kissed her again before walking over to sit at the table. "Bring me this delicious oatmeal you've made."

She knew he was being sarcastic, but her oatmeal really was good, and she was excited for him to try it. She'd added a generous amount of butter, cinnamon and brown sugar. She wasn't terribly fond of oatmeal, but it was an inexpensive breakfast, good for cold days, and when she'd put all of the extras on it, it was downright good.

She opened the oven and took out the toast she'd made to go with the oatmeal, piling it onto a plate. She served them both a generous helping of the oatmeal. She took him his cereal and the plate of toast before serving him his coffee. She got her own coffee and her oatmeal and went over to sit across from him.

He'd already eaten two pieces of toast by the time she sat down, but she could tell he hadn't even tried the oatmeal.

"My oatmeal really is good. Try some." She glared at him until he picked up his spoon.

"I was hoping for pancakes." He made a face like a petulant child as he held the spoon in front of him. He didn't want to eat oatmeal.

"You said you'd eat anything I cook," she said, frowning at him.

"Yes, but I didn't think you'd make oatmeal!" He ate what was on his spoon, his face changing as the flavor hit his tongue. "This is good!"

"I told you to trust me!" She shook her head. "I know what you like. If it's sweet, you'll devour it!"

Lars reached out and took her hand in his. "Thank you for learning my preferences and caring what they are. I still prefer pancakes, but this is a good breakfast for cold days."

She smiled. "I will try to make a variety of different things, but you'll get pancakes pretty regularly."

"That's all I ask."

WHILE HE WAS WORKING, Meg got the basement cleaned to her satisfaction and rearranged all the jars on the shelves so she'd know where everything was. The kitten played happily at her feet while she worked.

After she finished, she made lunch, and made a dozen muffins as a dessert for lunch and a snack for him to take in the afternoon. She didn't have any fresh fruit to use, so she made cinnamon muffins that had brown sugar and cinnamon topping.

Lunch was generous slices of ham, in a sandwich, warmed in the oven. She had a feeling Lars would enjoy that with the muffins.

She was still a bit puzzled by his change of heart, but she was pleased. He was acting as if he was courting her now and that was what she'd been after all along. He hadn't brought her flowers or any special candy, but his praise and holding her hand at breakfast had been just as good coming from him.

She was setting lunch on the table, right around half past twelve when he walked in the door for lunch. He waited until her hands were empty, grabbed her to him and kissed her, whispering words she hadn't realized she needed until that moment. "I missed you this morning."

The words surprised Lars, but he realized he'd been feeling them. When he stopped thinking of her as an enemy trying to take his wife's place in his heart, it became easy to care for her. She was cheerful, loving, and a hard-worker.

Meg wrapped her arms around his neck to pull him down for another kiss. "I missed you too. It was a long morning alone."

He just held her for a moment. "Stop wasting my time, woman! I'm hungry." The twinkle in his eye told her he was playing, and she was happy to find the playful side of him. He hadn't shown it much yet.

"Then sit down and eat, you big oaf. There's no one stopping you!" She winked as she said the words, so he would know she was teasing him back.

He chuckled, enjoying her playfulness. It was very different than his marriage with Olga had been. Once his first wife had lost a child, she'd become very sad, having a hard time caring about anything. She'd perked up every time she'd found out she was carrying another baby, and then become sadder than ever when she lost it. He knew through the last pregnancy that if she lost that baby, she would probably die with it. Her heart broke a bit more with each one.

He shook his head, pushing the sad memories away and sat down at the table, looking at the hot sandwich in front of him. "Is this the ham from last night?"

"Yes. I try to use up anything that's left before making something else. I'll make a soup tonight using beans, carrots and the hambone."

He took a bite of his sandwich, studying her as she flitted around getting everything onto the table. "Have you always been this frugal?"

Meg shrugged. "I guess so. I wasn't raised in a household with a lot of money. Often my mother would bring home what was left from her employer's table and make it into new meals for us. It's how I learned."

"I appreciate it. I have had many struggles with money, and a farmer never knows whether the crop will be a good one or a bad one. Making things stretch is good for us." At that moment, they didn't have money problems, but that could turn at any time. Better for her to always live as if they had nothing than always live as if they had plenty.

She watched him throughout the meal, enjoying his pleasure in simple things like sandwiches. She planned to bake more bread that afternoon, feeling like the bread they were eating was getting a bit stale, but he ate every bite without complaint.

When he finished, he pushed his chair back as if to get up, but she held up a hand, going to the work table and getting the muffins out from under a towel she'd placed over them. "Don't you want dessert?"

He looked down at the two muffins on a plate in front of him and smiled. "What is this?"

"Cinnamon muffins. Have you never had them?"

He shook his head. "They are not a Norwegian food." He pinched off a bite and put it into his mouth, his eyes closing as he savored the flavor. "These need milk."

She poured them each a glass of milk, and got a muffin for herself. She couldn't express how happy it made her when he liked what she made to eat. Was she falling in love with him?

She was startled by the thought. She'd only known him for a few days, most of which he'd been very sour toward her. Yes, he was handsome, but she didn't think of herself as a woman swayed by an attractive man.

He watched her, wondering at the emotions that were on her face. Something had stunned her and she seemed almost upset. "Is something wrong, Meg? Did I upset you somehow?"

She shook her head. "No, I'm fine." Her mother had once told her that she would know she was in love if she couldn't imagine a life without a man. She knew she could survive without him. Why, she could get a job teaching or doing any number of things. But she could no longer see her life without him.

Meg lost her appetite pushing the muffin away. What was she going to do? She loved him, and he still—well, he'd just quit thinking of her as the enemy. How in the world was she going to make him fall in love with her too? There was nothing worse than a one-sided love. Better if there had been no love at all.

She got up and started the dishes, doing them mechanically.

Lars was unsure of what had just happened, but he was suddenly worried. It was as if she had been lit by a candle from the moment he met her, and all of a sudden someone had blown the candle out. He didn't want to imagine life with her as melancholy as Olga had been. He couldn't live that way again.

He got up to leave, kissing her cheek on his way out the door.

"Wait!" she called.

He turned, hoping to see her face lit up like it usually was. Instead, she held out his lunch pail. "I put two muffins in there so you could have a snack later," she said, her voice mechanical.

He took the pail. "Thank you."

She nodded as he left to return to his work.

Chapter Nine

LARS WENT OUT TO THE barn carrying the lunch pail Meg had
given him. Something was wrong with her, and he didn't know what.
Already she was worming her way into his heart. Her upbeat attitude
made a difference for him after the sadness that permeated Olga for
years before her death.

He had taken on her sadness once she died, almost feeling as if it
was a vigil he must carry on to keep her alive in some way.

Yes, there had been necessary sadness right after her death, and after
the death of their son, but it was time for him to move on with his life.
Time for him to be happy. His sweet bride was so good for him, and he
knew he needed to do what he could to keep her happy.

He didn't think it could be the Dakota prairie that was bothering
her, because then she'd have been upset when he got there. No, it was
something to do with him. He wanted to get her a nice gift to make
her feel better, but it was a three hour trip into town and back by horse.
That was too far.

He saw one of the blocks of wood he kept there for his whittling
and picked it up, turning it over in his hand. He couldn't pick flowers
in November, but he could make her something just as nice. He found
a knife that he used to cut bales of hay for the horses and sat down on
a bale with his back to the barn wall. How long could it take to make a
sweet surprise for his bride?

He closed his eyes for a moment and thought about what he
wanted to make her and smiled. Yes, she would like it.

MEG DID HER CHORES in a bit of a daze that afternoon. How had she fallen in love so quickly? She'd thought she was more practical than that.

She baked a cake for him, knowing he would be thrilled for the sweet treat after supper. No longer was she willing to try to make him love her with food. No, she would wait for it to happen naturally if it ever did. But how could it? He obviously still loved his Olga, the woman he'd married young and emigrated with from Norway.

She sang softly as she worked, a song of unrequited love that her mother had always sung on days she was sad. It felt good to sing the old Irish tune, and she felt less alone in the world.

When the bread had been baked and the soup was boiling on the stove, she sat at the table in the kitchen darning all of her husband's socks. She couldn't find a single pair without a hole in them, and she'd already noticed he needed new boots. When he bought them, he would surely get blisters.

She wished she had some yarn so she could knit him some new socks, but that was something she would have to get from the mercantile in town. She wondered if Lars would let her take the wagon to get some yarn and some yard goods so she could start making Christmas presents for him.

The whole while she worked, she sang sad song after sad song, realizing they were making her feel better quickly. She had a voice that was clear and pretty, and she knew it, having taken many singing lessons from the pastor's wife of her church when she was younger. The lessons were grueling, but she'd been a willing pupil, always enjoying singing for her congregation.

She looked up when the door opened at five, thirty minutes earlier than he usually came in. She jumped up, dropping socks everywhere. "Oh, I'd have cleaned this up if I'd known you were coming home earlier than usual today. I'm so sorry!"

He shook his head. "You did nothing wrong. I—I spent the afternoon making you a gift instead of working."

Meg stared at him in disbelief. Why, Lars seemed almost shy to her, something she'd never seen from him. "You did?"

"Close your eyes," he said, seeming much younger than his years to her. It was almost as if he was—well, as if he was trying to court her. Was that possible?

She closed her eyes and waited, wondering what he could have possibly made her while he was outside all day. She felt a soft kiss brush across her lips, and she smiled. A kiss that sweet was a perfect gift.

He took her hand, watching her face to be certain she didn't open her eyes, and put his carving into it. "You can look now."

She held up the object, obviously wood, to see it. "Oh my," she whispered softly, her fingers tracing the small wooden cat. "You made this today?" She'd had no idea such an intricate carving could be made in such a short time. "Why, this is the work of a true artist."

Lars blushed a little at her praise. "I thought you might like something hand-carved by me."

She flew into his arms, hugging him tightly. "I love it. Thank you so much!"

She knew then that he was developing feelings for her. Maybe it wasn't love yet, but he wouldn't have gone out of his way to make her something so special if he hadn't cared at least a little.

She walked to the sink and put the small cat on the windowsill of the window she looked out while she did the dishes every day. "I'll treasure it always," she told him, a bright smile on her face.

He rubbed the back of his neck, a little embarrassed by her enthusiasm. "Ah—I'll go and milk the cows." He grabbed the bucket and walked outside, surprised by how much her happiness thrilled him.

As he walked he thought about her smile, and how he never again wanted to see her without it. And then it hit him. He loved her. Not in the way he'd loved Olga, because that love had faded when he'd had to hold her up during her sadness. He'd always loved her, up until the end, but he'd loved her more as a friend than a husband loving his wife.

Every time he looked at Meg, he realized how strong she was. He could see that she was a happy person deep inside. Olga had been given to fits of melancholy even before she'd lost the first baby. She'd wept copiously when they'd left the village where they'd both been born and raised.

No, his Meg would grieve the loss of a baby, as any woman would, but she wouldn't dwell on it the way Olga had. She wouldn't lose the ability to smile entirely.

When he went back to the house, he stood outside the door for a moment, trying to get his courage up. It was the first time he'd see her since realizing his love, and that made it more difficult for some reason.

Her pure sweet voice came through the door and he stood listening for a moment. The song she sang was in another language. Gaelic maybe? Whatever it was, the notes were beautiful. He'd had no idea she could sing that way. Was there anything his darling wife couldn't do? Other than deal with unruly children in a schoolhouse, of course.

He opened the door to her beautiful smile, the notes fading from her lips. "Supper's ready. Wash your hands and sit down, and I'll serve us."

He nodded, washing his hands and going to his spot across the table from her, nervous still.

She put a large bowl of soup on the table in front of him, and a loaf of fresh bread. "Every time you bake bread, and I come home and smell it filling the air, I want to get down at your feet and kiss them."

She laughed. "Instead of kissing my feet to thank me for the bread, you're welcome to kiss my lips or even my cheek. That would do just as well."

He chuckled, liberally slathering butter on a piece of bread. "Are you sure that's showing the depth of emotion I feel for you? I know it's not enough emotion for the bread."

She poured his milk before moving to sit across from him. "Just eat it. It makes me happy to see you enjoying something I've made for you."

While she ate her dinner, she felt something new between them. It wasn't just her newly realized feelings for him. It was knowing he cared for her as well. If he didn't, he wouldn't have made the cat for her. She glanced over at the wooden cat and smiled. He was courting her.

Maybe he didn't love her yet, but she thought it was possible for it to come if he cared enough to make her something frivolous. If he'd made her something useful for the house, it would have been something else entirely in her mind. But he made something that would just look pretty. She couldn't ask for more

He was thrilled by the cake, and she sat down with a large serving of it herself. He gazed at her plate with a grin. "You like sweets too!"

"Of course I do. I'm just not fond of pumpkin pie. I'll make it as often as you would like me to, though."

"Any other sweets you don't like? Just so I don't ask for them and force you to cook something you won't eat." He already knew she would do anything to make him happy. How God had known he needed her, he didn't know, but she was the woman he was meant to spend his life with. He could feel it.

After she'd finished the dishes, he caught her hand and pulled her down into his lap. He didn't know if he should be as nervous as he was. Would she send him off to his lonely room again?

He kissed her, his hands stroking her back. He couldn't let it get out of hand without knowing what her plan was. Finally, he broke off, resting his forehead against hers. "Are you sleeping with me or upstairs tonight?"

Meg took a deep breath. She knew what her answer needed to be. She loved him, and she was married to him. Was there any reason left to deny his husbandly rights? "I'll sleep with you."

"Thank you," he breathed reverently, getting to his feet, and taking her hand, leading her to his bedroom.

He knew she'd been in his room, because it was clean, but he hadn't been in there with her. It was different.

"I'm nervous," she whispered softly, unsure of what she was supposed to do.

He sat at the foot of the bed, catching her waist in his hands. "There's no reason to be. We'll take it as slow as you want."

She smiled, winding her fingers through his dark blond hair. "Thank you. I'm blessed to have you for a husband."

He pulled her down onto the bed, kissing her sweetly. "Just keep that in mind the next time I make you angry."

She laughed, pulling him down for another kiss. "I'll do my best."

Chapter Ten

THE SATURDAY BEFORE Christmas had Meg terribly excited. There was going to be a Christmas party at the church, and the pastor himself had found them when they'd gone into town for supplies, inviting them both.

"I know it's a far drive for you two, but it would be a good way for Margaret to get to know some of the local ladies."

Meg looked at Lars, trying not to get her hopes up. She wanted to go so badly, but she didn't know how he'd feel about it. He'd told her shortly after she arrived that he hadn't been to church since Olga and the baby had died.

Lars looked at Meg's face, knowing immediately she wanted to go, and not seeing a good reason to deny her. He did want her to be able to make friends with others in the area. She missed being around other women, although she never complained.

Meg was dressed in her prettiest Sunday dress for the church party. "It's starting to snow!"

Lars looked out the window, needing to be sure it wouldn't be a harsh snowfall, but it wasn't. It was just a light flurry. "Are you ready?" he asked. She looked prettier than he'd ever seen. Her skirt was a bright red, and she wore a pretty pink blouse with it. She had a red coat with a black trim to wear with it, and he knew he had the most beautiful bride in all of the Dakotas.

She nodded, putting her hands to the sides of her head to be sure her hair hadn't fallen from its carefully arranged bun when she put her red bonnet on. "I think so. Do I look all right?"

He grinned, pulling her to him and kissing her softly. "You didn't look kissed before, but you do now. That's important."

She laughed, pushing against his chest, but not really wanting him to let go of her just yet. "Why do I need to look kissed?"

"We can't have any of those other men around here thinking you're available. You, my dear Meg, are taken."

She shook her head. "No one else will look at me as you do. How could they? I look kissed now."

"I may have to kiss you before you go into the church again. Just to be sure."

"I might even ask you to kiss me again. I can't have my lips looking unkissed!"

Beth watched them from her vantage point in front of the stove, her eyes seeming to scold them for planning to leave her. Meg wished she didn't have to leave the kitten alone, but she knew she would be much better off at home. "Let me get my dish for the potluck, and we'll go."

"What are you taking?" he asked, trying to peek at the dish she'd just removed from the oven.

"Stop that! People are going to think I never feed you!"

He laughed. "You've had to take my pants out, so I think they'll know you've fed me." He patted his belly, not complaining a bit about the weight he'd gained since their marriage. He'd needed the extra pounds and wasn't a bit embarrassed that his wife cooked so well.

She had fashioned a quilted covering for the dish, so that it wouldn't cool too much on the way into town. She gripped it by the handles, stepping out into the snow. "It's so pretty!"

"You like snow?" he asked, though he already knew the answer. She had gone out and built a snowman and made snow angels with their first big snowfall of the year. He'd come home from work and wondered if she'd done anything at all while he'd been out, but the answer had been a resounding yes. The woman seemed incapable of sitting idle.

He helped her into the sleigh. The snow was just deep enough to make the sleigh necessary, and she'd been excited to travel in it. He'd hung jingle bells on the horses reins, knowing it would make her happy.

As they drove, she sang every Christmas carol she could think of, happy to be alive and celebrate Christmas. There would be a Christmas gift exchange at the church, and she'd made a small lap quilt for covering on cold winter nights, sitting by the fire, as well as two dozen cookies. Everything was wrapped together behind the seat of the sleigh.

She sat under the lap blanket that covered her and Lars, snuggling up against him. "I'm so excited to meet everyone. I don't think I've talked to more than three women since I came to marry you."

"I wanted to keep you all to myself," he told her with a grin, turning to kiss her forehead.

She sighed. "I love our house, but I do wish we had someone close by that I could be friends with."

"I do too." He didn't really care much for himself, but he did for her. She was everything to him, and if it would make her happy to have neighbors, then he wished they had them. The two months they'd been married had been the happiest time of his life.

When they got to the church, he helped her down, taking the dish from her. "You go in with this, and I'll get our present," he said.

She nodded, hurrying into the church and moving to put their dish on the long row of dishes the women had all brought for the pot luck. They'd been told to bring dishes and utensils enough for themselves, and a dish to share. That way everyone could take their own dirty dishes home to wash, and the woman would be able to join the festivities instead of having to spend all evening washing dishes.

She turned away from the dish, and she spotted a sprig of mistletoe hanging above the doorway. As soon as she saw it, she looked around to see if Lars had made it inside yet. When she didn't see him in the small crowd, she hurried over to wait for him in front of the door, loving the idea of kissing him under the mistletoe.

When Lars walked in, he frowned at Meg standing all alone beside the door. She'd wanted to go so badly, yet she wasn't even trying to talk to anyone. "Are you afraid to meet new people?" he asked. "Do you want me to introduce you?" She didn't seem the type to him to need to wait for an introduction, but he was willing to do it if she wanted.

Meg grinned up at him, pointing above his head to a piece of greenery. "Mistletoe," she said with a laugh.

He grinned. "So that's why you're over here by yourself. You're trying to force me to kiss you."

She nodded emphatically. "You can't escape it. You must do your duty and kiss me under the mistletoe."

He caught her by the waist and pulled her to him, kissing her thoroughly. After a moment he heard the applause start.

Meg giggled as he released her, and Lars smiled around at everyone. "My friends, this is my wife, Meg."

The women rushed over to greet Meg, while the men shook his hand. One older woman with blond hair and green eyes took Meg's elbow, ushering her off to the side of the room and away from Lars. "Oh, you're just what that man needed."

Meg smiled, happy for the compliment. "What makes you say that?"

"It's your smile. It's contagious. Everyone could see by the way he looked at you when he came into the room that you have touched his heart." The woman sighed. "I'm Belinda Martin. I'm the midwife around here."

Meg smiled. "I'm happy to meet you."

"I'm sure you'll need my help before too long."

Meg blushed. "Not yet, but soon I hope. Lars wants a son."

Belinda introduced her around and she had a wonderful time. It wasn't long before it was time to eat, and Lars came to lead her to the table.

"All the men are envying me tonight," he said with a smile.

She laughed. "And all the women envy me." She had rarely seen him dressed up, and she was startled by just how handsome he was, standing beside her in his black dress hat.

"Oh, I don't know about that." Honestly he didn't care if the other women envied her, because he knew he would never again have the desire to look at another. Meg filled his heart with so much love, there was no room for another woman.

They ate, talking to the people around them, and Meg was thrilled to learn a newly married couple had moved in just a couple miles south of them. "We could visit!" Meg exclaimed excitedly. "You should come over for tea some afternoon."

"Oh, I'd love to!" Alice, her new neighbor, told her. "We'll make arrangements before we leave tonight."

After all the food had been eaten, and the gifts exchanged, a man pulled out a fiddle, and the room filled with music. The tables were pushed out of the way, and Meg found herself pulled into her husband's arms. He danced her around the room, finally stopping under the mistletoe.

Meg's gaze went up to it, and she grinned. "You're not planning to kiss me *again*, are you?"

He cupped her face in his hands, lowering his lips to hers. "I plan to kiss you every day for as long as I live. I love you, Meg Borgen. I'm so glad you came here and married me."

Meg snuggled close to him. "I love you too, Lars. I was so worried you'd never be able to love me."

"Well, I never intended to, but how could I help it? When you find yourself married to the woman God made just for you, you can't keep fighting it forever."

Meg couldn't believe he loved her as she loved him, but it brought her heart joy. No longer would she feel as if she were a replacement wife. She was his bride, and she would love him forever.